LEGACY

BOOK 28

CERBERUS MC SERIES

Marie James

COPYRIGHT

CERBERUS MC

New to the Cerberus MC?

Each book is a **standalone** with a continuing subplot and can be read individually, but to get the most out of the series, it's best to read in order.

Kincaid: Cerberus MC Book 1
Kid: Cerberus MC Book 2
Shadow: Cerberus MC Book 3
Dominic: Cerberus MC Book 4
Snatch: Cerberus MC Book 5
Lawson: Cerberus MC Book 6
Hound: Cerberus MC Book 7
Griffin: Cerberus MC Book 8
Samson: Cerberus MC Book 9
Tug: Cerberus MC Book 10
Scooter: Cerberus MC Book 11
Cannon: Cerberus MC Book 12
Rocker: Cerberus MC Book 13
Colton: Cerberus MC Book 14
Drew: Cerberus MC Book 15
Jinx: Cerberus MC Book 16
Thumper: Cerberus MC Book 17
Apollo: Cerberus MC Book 18
Legend: Cerberus MC Book 19
Grinch: Cerberus MC Book 20
Harley: Cerberus MC Book 21
Landon: Cerberus MC Book 22
Spade: Cerberus MC Book 23
Aro: Cerberus MC Book 24
Boomer: Cerberus MC Book 25
Ugly: Cerberus MC Book 26
Bishop: Cerberus MC Book 27
Legacy: Cerberus MC Book 28
Stormy: Cerberus MC Book 29
Hemlock: Cerberus MC Book 30

Newton: Cerberus MC Book 31
Oracle: Cerberus MC Book 32
A Very Cerberus Christmas
Cerberus MC Box Set 1
Cerberus MC Box Set 2
Cerberus MC Box Set 3
Cerberus MC Box Set 4
Cerberus MC Box Set 5

SYNOPSIS

I never expected to see her again.

The connection we shared through her brother was severed when he died in combat.

Their parents were adamant that I never reach out to them again.

I forgot about the pact I made, my promise to make her mine if I wasn't married by thirty.

The only answer I had for her when she showed up with that handwritten note was no.

Only Devyn Malloy isn't the type to take no for an answer.

Cerberus welcomed her with open arms, but as that became enough for her, I realized it might not be enough for me...

PROLOGUE

LEGACY

11 Years Ago

My vision grows hazy as I lift my eyes to the horizon. I've been in a dreamlike state for the better part of two weeks. It's not that I'm in denial, but things still just don't seem real.

My eyes are dry, the only pair without tears in the very large gathering. I try not to feel anger at some of the sobbing people standing around. A lot of people would see that anger as misplaced. How could I have a clue who Vaughn touched in his lifetime? Maybe he had a relationship with the girl to my left. Maybe he knew the lady from the grocery store better than I realized.

But none of that is possible. Until two weeks ago, I spent literally a part of every single day of the last ten years with the guy. I went on vacation with his family. He went on vacation with mine. We knew everything about each other. I knew who he spoke with, who he spent time with, who he liked and disliked.

I knew he was missing home. I knew he was regretting listening to me in the first place. I knew he only joined the Marine Corps because I did. I made it sound so awesome, and as best friends, we didn't want to be separated.

Only now, instead of spending a handful of years to fulfill the obligation to my family I was raised to believe was required, I'll spend the rest of my life without him.

I swallow against the lump threatening to form in my throat, my dress blues suddenly scratchy against my skin. The irritation makes me want to reach for the letter again.

Every one of us was told to write one, to give it to someone we trust to deliver it if the unthinkable happened.

I almost scoff at the thought. The unthinkable—risking your life isn't so unthinkable when you head face-first into gunfire. Taking every precaution doesn't guarantee safety when the opposition is readily willing to die at all costs.

The preacher continues to speak, his words about Vaughn true and marked with his own pain and grief. He knew Vaughn as much as anyone who saw him nearly every Sunday, growing up, could. His words aren't generic the way many are at funerals, the officiant speaking from things told by family. It's as genuine as possible.

My best friend is gone, his life taken long before it should've been.

My platoon mates were grieving when I was given leave to attend today. They were quick to tell me it wasn't my fault. The chances of Vaughn losing his life on a random, routine scouting mission were statistically low.

Low.

I heard the word more times than I can count. Yet here I am, back home in Bumfuck, Nebraska, staring at the glossy black box that's holding less of my best friend than it did when we left home less than a year ago.

How could I have known that this would happen when I ended up with food poisoning that night and Vaughn took my place on patrol? A million things had to have lined up for this to occur.

It didn't help then, and it doesn't help now.

Mr. and Mrs. Malloy won't even look in my direction. They made it very clear yesterday that they blame me fully.

Being a Marine was never Vaughn's dream until I mentioned my requirement at twelve. Like everything else, my best friend fully committed to the idea. If I was going, he was going too. I didn't even have to ask. It was a foregone conclusion. Where I went, he went, and vice versa. Our lives had been like that since the day we met when my family moved to Broken Bow the summer before third grade.

I clench my hands to keep from reaching for the letter stuffed in my pocket. The tone of it doesn't match the emotions of the group. It's lively and upbeat, his requests childish and not carrying the weight of him actually being gone. He asks me to erase his browser history because there's no need for his mom to know he's into anime porn. He demanded that I tell Adrienne that he never really liked her. Something I know is a lie because he spoke of her often. The girl backed out of prom a week before the big day and it has chapped his ass every day since.

The final part of the letter, the only thing that was serious, was less of a request and more of an assumption. He told me to continue to love his family the way I always have. They saw me as a son, and it wasn't fair for them to lose both of theirs, unless, of course, we both died together. Honestly, he thought that's what would happen because we did everything together.

The joke's on me, however, because I'm the one left behind. I'm the one who was told last night that I'm a murderer. That it's my fault Vaughn is gone. Mrs. Malloy told me she wished I never would've knocked on their door that day to see if the boy I saw while moving in across the street could play. She was sobbing when she said she wished it were me instead of him.

Doesn't she know that there hasn't been a single day in the last two weeks that I haven't wished the same?

I feel empty, soulless, lost.

A literal part of me died that day, and honestly, I don't know if I want it back. I don't need that piece of me that needs others in my life. The loss of them is too much of a burden to bear.

I keep my eyes on the grieving Malloy family as the preacher asks everyone to bow their heads for a final prayer. Mrs. Malloy grips her husband's hands tight in her lap, her shoulders shaking from her sobs. Silent tears streak down the man's face. I can tell he's trying to be strong for his wife, but he's close to losing it as well.

Tiny feet in lace-ruffled socks and black shoes kick back and forth on Mr. Malloy's left. Devyn only got six short years with her brother. Guilt for my role in all of this swims inside of me as I look at her innocent face.

She sees me watching her, her cheeks turning up into a smile. She lifts her hand, giving me a little wave, her fingers gripping one of those journals she's always carrying around with her.

I nod at her in return. She doesn't blame me simply because she's too young to understand. I have no doubt her parents will share their views with her, making it impossible to satisfy my best friend's last wishes. His family no longer loves me like a son because I'm the reason they lost theirs. I can't look after them the way he wanted me to. I can't make sure Devyn doesn't date until she's thirty, nor help his dad with the old Pontiac in the garage he was too busy in high school to help rebuild. Not being welcome in their home means I won't be around to offer to till Mrs. Malloy's backyard garden because Mr. Malloy's back is too bad from a previous at-work injury to help her with it.

As the preacher says amen, I have to walk away. The last thing I want is for his parents to notice me in the crowd. I've caused them enough grief, and they demanded I stay away today, even knowing I couldn't.

I lost my best friend two weeks ago, but today, I walk away from three more people I truly love.

1

Devyn

I'm a chicken. The biggest coward who ever walked the earth.

Instead of going downstairs and telling my parents the truth, I'm in my room, sitting on the floor, going through all my things in preparation for leaving for college tomorrow. At least that's what my parents believe—both that I'm packing my necessities and going to college.

I lied months ago about being accepted to the University of Nebraska, Omaha. Omaha is over three hours away from home, and at the time, I figured I could just move and use the money I've earned working at one of the dollar stores in town to get a small apartment. I could keep the lie up for four years because my parents aren't exactly the type of people to travel for any reason. Since they couldn't be bothered to attend any school functions of mine growing up, other than my graduation, I didn't figure they'd get involved in any trips to the university.

I nearly fell over last night when they said they'd both taken off work to make sure I made it to campus safely. Dad offered to bring his small picture-hanging kit in case I wanted to hang anything on my dorm room walls. Mom bought a small rug for my bedside because she didn't want my feet getting cold. The behavior of both of them was unusual. They've never really concerned themselves with my daily life other than to make sure there was food in the fridge.

It's been like that my whole life, making me a very self-sufficient person. I cook and I shop for myself now that I'm old enough. I'm not exactly neglected. They don't expect me to pay for my necessities, but I've never experienced a shopping trip with my mom. Until I was old enough to drive, my parents always brought things they bought home on their way back from work.

The buzz of the lawn mower in the backyard jolts me back to reality, and I forgo my fake packing. I wish I had the courage to tell my parents the truth, as I stand and cross the room to the singular window. I keep to the side, out of sight, and look down on Seb as he pushes the mower across the lawn. He's been mowing the lawn for my parents for years. I hate the crush I had on him, the one that led to flirting, which led to the night we spent together over Christmas break. He was home for college, and I was feeling unseen and neglected by everyone in my life.

Wanting to escape my life, I told him I loved him after, the warmth of his skin against mine giving me the courage that was always out of reach until that moment. Like any man in his right mind would do, he told me what happened between us was a mistake. I can't blame him for being the sane one in the moment. I knew then I didn't love him, but I saw him as a way out of Broken Bow. Rightfully so, he got dressed and scurried away like a mouse caught in the kitchen in the middle of the night. We haven't spoken since. As I watch him mow, he doesn't once look up at my window despite him having done it often last summer. In part, that's what gave me the courage to approach him. He was always the older guy across the street, the one out of reach because of the three-year difference in our ages. He was a senior when I was a freshman and completely untouchable.

I left the curtain closed, the stiff fabric falling from my fingers, relegating me right back to a world filled with artificial light in a home I've never really felt love in.

Sighing, I retake my place inside of my small closet and pull a box close to me. A wave of nostalgia hits me as I pull the flaps open to reveal several journals.

I'm known for always having one with me. I've carried them my entire life. Since I have nothing but time on my hands, I start from the very first one. I recall labeling each of them as I got older. It was done in a chaotic time in my life, and I felt like having control over this was, in part, having control over uncontrollable things in my life.

The first one was from kindergarten. I can practically hear my teacher when she told the class that writing every day would make us superstars. She smiled at me every time she saw me with a notebook in my hands. I know now I did it because I craved her approval.

My cheeks swell, a small smile playing on my lips as I flip through the pages of crude drawings and letters of the alphabet I practiced relentlessly. I run my fingers over the stick figure family of five. Everyone had a wide smile on their faces, and it makes me wish I'd known at the time to write the dates down.

I had a brother once upon a time. I know the second boy in the drawing was my brother's best friend, Emmett Wilson. They were inseparable, and I fought to spend time with them as often as I could. But the nearly twelve-year age difference meant they were practically grown before I was capable of forming memories of them.

Vaughn died when I was six, a casualty of a war my parents swear he never should've gotten involved in. They blamed his best friend for joining the Marine Corps in the first place, but my earliest memories of my brother involved him being excited about traveling the world and defending his country. The plaque on the wall at my school declares my brother a hero, but my parents claim to this day that he died because of Emmett's selfishness.

I used to hate the man, but as I've gotten a little older, I know what it's like to want to leave this small town. I know what it's like to consider all the options in order to walk away and never look back. Maybe that's what Vaughn felt as well. Maybe Emmett made the suggestion of joining the Marine Corps, but I doubt the man bribed him into joining.

A pattern begins where I stop writing my name and begin writing Vaughn's. Several pages later, I come across Emmett's name, the first one on the page written in perfect block letters, followed by a child's handwriting, trying to mimic it. He had to have written this in here all those years ago.

I flip the page, the rough alphabet letters transforming into hearts. I don't recall having a crush on Emmett Wilson, but the evidence of it is right before my eyes.

I run my finger over the heavy-handed words. *I'll marry Devyn Malloy when I'm 30.*

My name is written in nearly illegible cursive. His signature written under the declaration is nearly as impossible to read.

I close my eyes, trying to recall that day, but the memories are just too old. Maybe I was just too young for them to stick.

I flip the page again, reading other promises made. Vaughn promising me he'll take me to the store for candy under the stipulation that I leave him alone for three hours. My mom promising me the new My Little Pony toy. Dad promising me I could stay up late if I helped clean the garage.

Although I can't recall any of these in detail, I do remember my dad saying he thought I'd grow up to be a lawyer like him since I seemed so fond of contracts.

It couldn't be further from the truth.

I continue to flip, seeing the worst drawing of a three-headed dog, the words *Cerberus MC* written under it. I can tell I attempted to draw the insignia of the organization Emmett and Vaughn spoke of often, the evidence on the pages rather than a genuine memory in my head.

The next journal shows a family of three, both Vaughn and Emmett gone from our lives. The faces are no longer smiling, and instead of being stick figures, they're wearing clothes.

I owe that to an episode of my favorite shows growing up. The stylish middle school girls held a fashion show for their school, and it began my obsession with clothes. Maybe I wanted my parents to see me the way their parents did. They were so supportive and always had smiles on their faces despite the shenanigans their daughters got up to.

I made good grades and stayed out of trouble. Although there were times they told me I did a good job, it was never done with enthusiasm. I know they love me in their own ways, but unfortunately, those ways were never bold and loud, and sometimes I needed that from them.

In high school, my grades slipped, and they didn't seem to notice.

Instead of staying involved in school-sanctioned activities, I got a job, praying that they'd care more if I lessened their burden. The only thing they ever did to show they cared about me at all was leaving the porch light on the nights I had to work after dark.

Instead of continuing my trip down memory lane, I grab my phone and open one of my social media apps, typing in my brother's name. I don't do this often, but nothing has changed since the last time I did. I swipe in reverse chronological order, reading the posts I've read before. The last one was from a couple years ago, my deceased brother having been tagged in posts made by classmates as they shared memories from many years prior.

Vaughn was always smiling, always happy, always standing right beside his best friend.

My finger hovers over Emmett's name. According to my parents, I'm supposed to hate the man who got my only brother killed. Logically, I know it wasn't Emmett's fault. He didn't plant the bomb that took Vaughn's life. Vaughn wasn't forced or coerced into joining the Marine Corps. But there's still that voice in the back of my head from my childhood that whispers that if Vaughn had never met Emmett, he'd still be around today. Those voices sound eerily like my mother. Although she hasn't mentioned the man's name in years out loud to me, I know she still blames Emmett for Vaughn's death, as if he were the one to end it himself.

I press my finger against the man's name, keeping my eyes closed as his page populates.

His posts are sporadic, the last one from over six months ago.

LEGACY is emblazoned on the patch adorning his crisp leather vest. His smile is wide, the corners of his eyes marked with a handful of wrinkles.

The post declares, *Dreams do come true.*

The location is marked as New Mexico. I know without having to do further research that he landed a job with Cerberus MC, making his and Vaughn's wishes come true.

That bitterness that belongs solely to my parents once again threatens to seep inside of me, and I have to exit the app to keep it from swallowing me whole. I told myself years ago that I wouldn't let that toxicity take over my life. I deserved more than what I got from my parents. That's on them, not on Emmett Wilson.

2

LEGACY

"Nervous?" Grinch asks, a knowing look in his eyes as he adjusts one of the straps on his bullet-resistant vest.

"No," I lie as I recheck the handgun on my hip to make sure it's in full working order for the fifth time since I holstered it.

"It's okay to be nervous," my team lead says. "I was nervous my first time out."

"This isn't my first time out," I remind him.

"It's your first time out with Cerberus," he challenges.

"I went to Lindell with the team," I tell him.

"That isn't exactly the same thing," Grinch says.

I frown at the man. "Are you purposely trying to psych me out or something?"

"I just need your head on your shoulders and your mind in the right place."

I've been a member of the Cerberus MC for seven months. Shortly after we arrived, one of the guys who came in with me was drugged, and what ensued was utter fucking chaos. There was an accusation that one of the other Cerberus members was involved with the murder of a local woman, only for it to be discovered there was a serial killer on the loose. Bishop was drugged too and ended up in a fucking coma.

Bishop, Stormy, and I haven't had the most routine introduction to the club. We've gone through months of mental health testing on top of the already strenuous requirements Cerberus required us to meet before joining. We haven't been singled out. Every team member has the same requirements, but it's left us grounded, not doing any fieldwork until now.

Even so, the teams are now staggered, only two going out at a time. I'm on team C with Grinch as our leader. Legend, Rivet, Scooter, and Boomer are also on this team.

"My head is in the right place," I assure him.

I know that the adrenaline pumping through my veins is a natural response to what I know we're facing. Being a hundred percent calm right now would only be possible for an insane person. Each time you're faced with a possible life-altering situation, you should be a little nervous. The heightened senses are helpful in most cases. You can see a little better, hear a little better, read things faster. It's basic survival instinct.

"No concerns?" Grinch asks.

"None," I tell him.

I know that if I had them, I wouldn't be penalized for voicing them. It's something that was drilled into our heads with the extra training we've been doing in recent months. We're more valuable to Cerberus than any given mission we've been assigned to. If we aren't feeling it, we need to let them know.

They nearly lost Aro last year, and they aren't willing to endanger our lives any more than necessary. Every precaution is taken. We're outfitted with the best weapons and gear money can buy.

"Good to hear," Grinch says, finally accepting that I'm ready to go. "You're behind Scooter."

I nod, taking a deep breath and releasing it slowly.

"Let's go ring some fucking bells," he growls to the rest of the team as he walks around to the passenger side of the armored SUV. It isn't exactly a SWAT type vehicle, and it probably wouldn't withstand an IED, but it's mostly bulletproof and could probably run through a house without hesitation. I know not to put all my trust in it. I know from firsthand experience that bombs have a way of being unpredictable.

The ride to the compound is silent, and I put all my focus into not bouncing my knee up and down as we draw closer.

Team A, led by Hound, is in the SUV ahead of us. They're the front entry team. Team C would normally be the rear entry team, but the compound we're heading to only has one way in. It makes it more dangerous because it means that the men we're going to be facing will be like caged animals. They have no means of escape. It's kill or be killed, and I don't doubt these lowlife pieces of shit would do anything to stay alive.

We park a quarter mile away, traveling on foot to the compound. Max, our IT specialist back in New Mexico, has somehow managed to work some magic, making the electronics the traffickers have useless. He's been having them glitch off and on for the better part of a week, with the hope that they're more annoyed and less suspicious when they go out fifteen minutes before Hound's team breaches the front door.

We hit the compound in the early morning hours, the first Cerberus member crossing the threshold at exactly 3:42 a.m. as planned. The time of day is important. Most people will be asleep, making them vulnerable. But it's always a gamble with places like this because they host visitors with sick-and-twisted needs at all hours of the day and night.

The sound of limited gunfire echoes through our comms, the Cerberus members rattling off as they clear each room. We still haven't been given the go-ahead to enter. We knew there was a real chance that our team would never even enter the tiny compound. Doing so while there were still men to take down would mean that Team A ran into a problem, and none of us wanted that.

The compound consists of five rooms total, including the bathroom and kitchen. I've been told it's one of the smaller places we'll deal with. As Hound informs us through his mic that the house is clear, I feel a little disappointed, like I donned all of this gear for nothing.

I shove that feeling down because it means that every Cerberus member is safe and unharmed. That's the best outcome we could hope for.

"Two women, one small boy," Apollo says.

"He's asking for his mother," Hound says. *"These two women aren't her."*

There's no damn telling where this boy's mother is. The men who abduct people aren't exactly concerned with keeping family members together. They send them where they're more likely to make the most money.

I stand back, keeping the nose of my assault rifle angled at the ground as the two women and little boy are escorted from the house. Their stares are blank, the abuse they've endured too debilitating to feel an ounce of happiness at being rescued. Hell, I wouldn't doubt if they aren't imagining they're just being taken by a stronger cartel, unbelieving that they're finally free of the torture and abuse.

I've seen a lot of pain and suffering during my time in the Corps, but nothing has prepared me for what I see inside this small house. I've been a witness to squalor and poverty on levels I never knew imaginable until the Marine Corps. I saw people doing their best with nearly nothing, living with dirt floors, and nothing more than what would equate to weeds from the yard to eat while I was in the Middle East. But the chains on the walls, the blood spilled on the floor, not belonging to the men Hound's team took down, are eye-opening.

"This isn't as bad as it will get," Rivet says as she walks closer to me.

I nod, knowing she's right.

We've gone over many of the past cases Cerberus has been involved in. Kincaid and the older guys who started the club didn't want us to be surprised. They didn't want us to let emotions get the better of us. They wanted to make us aware of what we're facing, wanted to know if we thought we could handle it, and they were always adamant that it's always worse in person.

I help Legend wrap one of the dead guys' bodies in a blanket from the bed and carry him out of the house.

Hound is speaking with an official from the closest town. He was the one who called and reported this house. Tears mark his face as Hound gives him the news. His daughter was not inside.

I've heard more than one conversation leading up to this infiltration tonight. The man who reported his daughter's abduction and pointed to this place as being responsible for taking her knew about it for years. In fact, intel says he's been getting kickbacks from the organization running this place for quite a while. When he demanded more money for his silence, his daughter went missing. He, of course, didn't admit any of this to Cerberus when requesting our help, but Max is very good at finding shit out.

The woman didn't deserve to be punished for his crimes, but the families aren't ever safe. Life isn't valuable to these people. This man is just as culpable for his daughter's abduction as he is for every woman, man, and child who has been cycled through this place.

I turn my attention back to the small house, watching as Harley and Scooter carry another man's body from inside.

3

Devyn

I shake my hands out as I descend the stairs, nervousness running through every extremity.

I didn't sleep last night. I couldn't shut my mind off. The lies I told months ago have come back to haunt me.

As I enter the kitchen, finding both my parents in there despite them normally avoiding each other at all costs, I still haven't decided if I'll tell them the truth now or wait until we all arrive on campus.

Maybe I'll be able to convince them that there was some sort of mix-up, and the college lost my information and gave my room to someone else. This is the problem with lying. You always have to tell more lies to cover up the first one. It compounds and builds until your entire life is a lie.

My parents haven't been very active in my life, but one thing they've been adamant about is that my life's goal of being a fashion designer isn't something they support. They disregarded my dreams, as if I asked for ice cream for dinner rather than wanting to eat grilled chicken and steamed vegetables.

"There's no money in fashion," my mother said dismissively five years ago when I spoke of my dream. I wanted to choose Home Economics over advanced accounting because there was a chance we'd eventually use a sewing machine.

I took the classes she wanted and worked on my fashion projects on my own because I never wanted to disappoint them.

They rehomed Vaughn's dog after he died because the sight of her was just too hard for them to deal with. As a young child, I felt as if I were just as disposable, and I never wanted to rock the boat. I didn't want to be shipped off or traded because I made their lives difficult.

Neither parent looks up at me when I enter the room, but there's a heaviness in the air. It's all too familiar. I can't recall a single loving moment between my parents other than the crude drawings in my journal. I imagine they fell apart after my brother's death, but it leaves me wishing I could remember happier times. I have no idea why they've even stayed together. My mother now stays in the room that was Vaughn's, and I rarely see them speak to each other. It's as if they're independently living in their own worlds, and this house just happens to be the place those worlds overlap.

"I'm not going to college," I blurt.

My mother turns around from her spot in front of the sink. From my periphery, I see my father look up from his iPad.

"Yes, you are," he says simply.

"I didn't even apply to the University of Nebraska. I lied."

"We know," Dad says, his voice devoid of any emotion. "My check was sent back six weeks ago with a letter stating there was a mistake because there wasn't a Devyn Malloy accepted."

"You knew?" I challenge, somehow feeling betrayed even though I was the one who lied in the first place.

My father drops his eyes back to whatever he was reading.

"I guess you'll just have to go to the local college," Mom says, turning the water back on to finish her breakfast dishes.

By local college, they mean the community college that's over an hour and a half away.

"And if I don't?" I snap, the tone in my voice unfamiliar.

I stare down at my hands, feeling like a complete failure as Mom turns the water in the sink off once again.

"You go to college or you leave," Dad says, his eyes still on his iPad.

"L-leave?" I manage.

"As in move out," Mom says. I wonder if they had a conversation about being a united front.

"You'll kick me out if I don't go to college?"

Mom's lips form a flat line, a hint of annoyance in her eyes.

"What if I go to fashion school?"

"Not an option," Dad says. "You'll get a degree in something useful."

"Or I'll be homeless?" I argue.

Only now does he look up at me. "It's your choice."

I know arguing with them would be a waste of time. There's never been a compromise where my parents are concerned. It's their way or no way. They don't care enough to argue. They never have. Their fight left them the day they got the call about Vaughn dying.

I don't give them an answer before leaving the kitchen and heading back up to my room.

I grab my phone and press the first contact.

"What did they say?" my best friend Quincy asks the second the call connects.

She knew I was heading down there to confess from our conversation earlier this morning.

I sigh before responding. "They told me I can go to college or leave."

Silence fills the line.

"Quince?"

"Seriously?" she says, disbelief in her tone.

"Yep," I confirm as I drop back onto my bed, my eyes angled up at the ceiling.

"I don't understand," she whispers, as if we're telling each other a secret.

"That's because you have two moms who love you more than anything in the world. We aren't the same."

"I'm so sorry," she says. I know she hates the way my parents are, as much as she feels grateful she was adopted by two women who love her dearly.

I don't begrudge her for the life she has. I just wish mine looked a little more like hers and much less like mine.

"What are you going to do?"

I wish I was bold enough to tell her that I'm going to pack all my things and leave. That living on my own and struggling all my life would be better than being stuck in some stupid class learning things that will only advance me in life and has no hope of making me happy, but I'm a reasonable person.

"I guess I'm going to register for classes at the community college," I mutter.

"In North Platte? It's over an hour away."

"I know." I lift my hand to my forehead, the threat of a headache pressing against my skull.

"Maybe you can get all online classes."

"Maybe," I say, thinking that's just as bad as driving so far and sitting in class.

I'd be less likely to keep my focus sitting in my room, but the energy it would take to go to class everyday doesn't sound very appealing at all either.

"Wanna meet for coffee later?"

She's silent once again.

"Quince?"

"I'm moving into my dorm today," she reminds me.

She's the only reason I knew anything about certain dates for the University of Nebraska. Where I lied about going to college, my best friend actually got in. As adamant as I've been about being a fashion designer, she's been the same way about being a Maverick.

"Maybe it's not too late to get in."

"Quince," I groan.

"I know, I know," she says. "The core classes would be a waste of time."

I never wanted to sit through another math or history class again. The only math and history I wanted to endure would be the math that came along with pattern making and the history of fashion trends.

"I'll figure something out."

When I expect her to offer the floor of her dorm room, she tells me that she has to go instead. I love my best friend, but she's never quite understood why I won't just go to college like a normal eighteen-year-old. Once she even agreed that maybe my parents were right about wanting me to have a safer degree, but she was quick to tell me that she knew I could make it as a designer.

I let it slide at the time. It's hard for someone who has such huge goals in life to understand that I just want to be happy. That meant doing something that made me happy, not getting stuck in some rat race and hoping for change later in life.

I didn't want to be an attorney like my dad or a corporate executive like my mother. They're miserable in their lives. Despite a lot of that having to do with Vaughn's death, they never find joy in anything.

"Have a safe trip," I tell her.

"Let me know what you decide," she says, ending the call a second later.

"If only I can figure that out for myself," I mutter into the empty room.

4

LEGACY

"What about strippers?" Stormy asks, a wide smile on his face.

"Not really my thing," I say, incapable of not smiling at how excited he seems about the idea. "But now I know what you'd like for your birthday."

"That new place down on main opened up a few weeks ago," Stormy says, still stuck on the stripper idea.

"Got shut down on their second day open," Boomer says.

"Underaged girls," his boyfriend Drake says, scrunching his nose in disgust.

"Gross," Stormy says, and I mumble my agreement. "So no strippers. What do you want?"

"Is being left the hell alone an option?" I ask.

"Come on, man," Stormy grumbles. "Birthdays are awesome."

It's mostly true. I had eighteen great birthdays, but Vaughn died on my nineteenth. I've avoided that day as much as possible since. They don't know that, however, and I have no intention of opening that can of worms.

I shared some of my history with Bishop, but I haven't spoken to these other guys about it. Those confessions came during a "whose life is worse" conversation with the guy who got drugged by a serial killer and lost five years of his memories. By the time we were both done complaining about our lives, we still couldn't decide who had the shittier end of the stick.

"The party is fine," I say when he makes it clear he's not going to leave it alone.

"The club party?" Stormy looks disgusted once again. "Everyone will be at those. We can't really celebrate the right way in front of kids."

"I think," I begin, wanting to change the subject, "that the bulletin board is a stupid idea."

"Let my wife hear you say that," Kincaid says as he enters the kitchen. "Emmalyn worked hard on that."

"She just wants everyone to stay up to date on what's going on in the clubhouse," Boomer says in Em's defense.

"Nothing against Em," I say quickly.

I don't exactly oppose the bulletin board, but the fact that everyone now knows when my birthday is, is because she posts all the important dates there. They have no idea of knowing that the date is a trigger for me. Besides, it's been eleven years. Vaughn's death should have a duller edge to it than it does, shouldn't it?

"We can head to *Jake's* and drink a few beers," I offer.

"Find some hot chicks," Stormy adds, his face showing a little more joy now that I've offered a better solution than a club party. "Maybe score with someone interested in a threesome."

Kincaid chuckles from across the room. I have no doubt the man was a tomcat when he was younger, but he's a hundred and fifty percent dedicated to his wife now.

"I'm not interested in a threesome," I mutter, immediately rejecting the idea.

"You've never had one?" Stormy asks, a challenge in his voice. He snaps his fingers as if he just came up with the best idea ever. "I know exactly what to get you."

"I don't want a threesome for my birthday," I say. It seems like he's filled in between the lines I've drawn, and I don't want to end up in a seriously awkward situation. "Stormy!"

He doesn't turn back around in his rush to leave the room.

"I swear if he brings two girls to my room," I mutter.

Drake chuckles, drawing my attention to him.

"What?"

He shakes his head. "I don't think he was considering two girls for you."

I tilt my head, it taking a little too long for me to figure out that he meant Stormy has it in his mind that we would share a woman.

"Not a fucking chance," I snap. "No offense."

"None taken," Drake says. "Everyone has their own things they're into."

"I'm not into group sex," I clarify, making the man laugh once again.

"It's not for everyone," Tug says as he enters the room with half of his triad, Max.

"That's my niece you're talking about," Kincaid says, but there's still a playfulness to his tone. "Meeting in two hours for room assignments."

"I can't believe how okay he is with what you guys get up to," I say when Max takes a seat across from me.

"Don't yuck my yum, man," our IT specialist says, a wide grin on his face as he looks past me to Tug.

I hold my hands up near my ears. "Sorry."

I know there was probably judgment in my tone, but it wasn't intentional. I don't care what anyone else does, but my temper has been getting shorter recently. I fucking hate this time of year, and it has nothing to do with the threat of fall and seasonal depression.

Like always, it makes me think of Vaughn. Something I've been doing more and more of since joining Cerberus. Ending up here was always our goal. My obligation to the military was just that, an obligation. I got my nickname because every generation in my family, for as long as anyone could recall, had someone who served in the Marine Corps. My mother brags about being able to trace that lineage back to the birth of the Corps during the American Revolution. It was a given that I'd join, but I only wanted to serve my expected four years. This clubhouse was always my goal. Vaughn and I talked about it often. We had our futures planned out. Not once in the time leading up to us leaving for the Corps did I consider one of us wouldn't make it. We left Broken Bow that day, right after graduation, with stars in our eyes, a naivety that lasted until the day our boots hit the sand in Qatar.

It only took a week before Vaughn confessed that he was terrified and that he made the wrong choice. He never blamed me. I don't even know if he remembers that it was my idea and not his with how gung-ho he was about defending his country. We weren't privileged to the politics and in-fighting until we were. None of that was mentioned by my father or my granddad. I don't know if they unintentionally didn't tell us when they were reliving those days through stories or if they purposely left it out in order to keep us in the dark. I felt betrayed by the men I looked up to. But after twelve years in the Corps, I realized that there are certain things you never talk about with others. There are things I know, things I experienced, that will never leave my lips. I know every man and woman in Cerberus feels exactly the same way.

"I bet we get to have one of the newer rooms," Boomer says, rubbing his hands together.

"Think it's required?" I ask, not looking forward to packing up all my stuff and moving it to the recent addition.

"Have you not used one of the showers in the new rooms?" Boomer asks, his cheeks pinking when Drake chuckles.

"You have?" I challenge, still a little delayed in understanding. "Never mind, don't answer that. I thought you two were staying at *Jake's*."

Drake lives in the apartment above the bar, and Boomer stays there more often than he does here most nights.

"Not if we're offered one of the new rooms here," Boomer says. "Like I said, the showers are amazing."

I turn my attention away from them as Drake leans closer and whispers something in his ear.

Happiness just pours out of people around here, and it makes me feel like my guilt and irritation just drags people down. I stand from the table, thinking that a few miles on one of the treadmills in the clubhouse gym sounds like a good idea.

"Didn't mean to run you off," Boomer says. "I did the plumbing in the bathrooms, remember? I had to make sure they were working correctly."

I smile at him, wanting to apologize for making things weird, but I decide that would be even weirder.

"It's all good," I say before leaving the room, wondering if they're going to think I have a problem with same-sex relationships with how I acted.

I don't have a problem with anyone. I'm very live and let live. I always have been. Drake and Boomer's relationship is no different from Kincaid and Emmalyn's as far as I'm concerned. I'm glad for anyone who has found happiness. I'm also aware that I'll never be one of those guys. It isn't in the cards for me.

There was nothing sexual between Vaughn and me, but I loved that guy like a brother. Losing someone you love that much leaves wounds that never truly heal. I couldn't put myself in a situation like that. I don't know if I'd survive another loss like that.

Since I'm also the kind of guy who never wanted to just screw around with women, it's posed a conundrum in my life. I have sex. I'm not celibate or anything. Hell, I've had one-night stands on occasion, but I'm not like Stormy whose whole view on women is that they're fun and meant to go home at the end of the night.

I'm more likely to nurture a relationship. In the end, I always end up hurting people when I can't fully commit. It's quite possibly my worst character flaw. It makes me a wuss because I'm afraid of getting hurt.

I try to keep my mind off the coming dates and focus more on the possibility that I may have to switch rooms. It's not like I'd argue. If Kincaid says we're moving, then so be it. But at the rate people are moving out, the new extension seems to be a waste of time.

We have three new guys coming in soon, but since Bishop moved out to live with Sunshine and her son, there's more than enough room in the older part of the clubhouse.

People are dropping like flies around here. Well, they're finding their happily ever afters and building houses on Cerberus property.

I shudder as I head outside to the gym. The thought of finding true love makes my skin crawl. Marriage and kids are just as bad. It's something I thought I'd end up with when I was younger, although I never made any real plans for it. That's just what people do, right? They grow up and get married. They buy a house and have a few kids.

But sometimes the people they love die. Sometimes the wife and kids get abducted and sold into sexual slavery. I'd much rather live a life of solitude than have to suffer something like that.

I climb on the treadmill, using all my energy to focus on my feet pounding on the belt. I'm able to clear my mind for half an hour before the memories slip back in.

5

Devyn

"It looks like that thing weighs a hundred pounds," Quincy says as I struggle to lift the suitcase into the back seat of her car.

"Don't offer to help or anything," I snap, irritated at the world right now.

Before she can open the driver's side door and climb out to help, I get the stupid thing situated.

I drop into the passenger seat, my heart racing as if I'm doing something illegal.

"I still don't know why you don't take your car."

"I wouldn't put it past my parents to report it as stolen," I mutter as she pulls away from the curb.

"They gave you the ultimatum. Go to college or leave. They can't really be upset you chose to leave."

"Correction," I say, holding up a finger. "I tried the school thing."

"For two months," Quincy clarifies.

"And that was long enough for me to know I'm not the type of person who goes to a traditional college. They aren't for everyone, you know."

"You sound like a technical school ad," she says.

I might have read a lot of research on different types of learning environments, but it didn't change what I had to do.

"The car is in my parents' names," I remind her, wanting to get off the subject of my less-than-stellar recent choices. "Plus, I don't want anything they gave me. I need to make it on my own."

She looks over her shoulder at the suitcase. "So you paid for everything in that suitcase? It sounded like you packed everything in there."

"I brought my sewing machine and my favorite clothes."

When we coast to a red light, she turns her full attention to me.

"You're leaving home for good, and you pack a sewing machine instead of necessities?"

I glare at her. "Have you not been paying attention? The sewing machine is a necessity. Besides, I worked my ass off to earn the money to buy it. I couldn't leave it behind."

"And how much money do you have for this adventure?"

"Enough."

She rolls her eyes. She was with me six months ago when I bought that sewing machine. She knows it depleted most of my savings.

"I want to go on record," she begins as she refocuses her attention back on the road when the light turns green. "I think this is a horrible idea."

"I appreciate your support."

"I'm your best friend, Devyn. I'm allowed to speak up when I think you're doing something dangerous."

I shift in my seat, my arms folding together defensively. "Did you tell your moms?"

She shakes her head. "I haven't, but I think I should. I know they'd let you stay there until—"

"Until what, Quince? Until I find a better paying job? Until I can afford to live on my own? Until I hate myself enough to go back to college so my parents will let me come back home?"

"That's not fair. I'm only concerned because I love you."

"I know." My words are a grumble.

I'm well aware that what I've chosen to do is dangerous. These aren't the best times for a young woman to travel halfway across the continent on her own. I watch the news. I know dangers lurk everywhere.

"What did they say when you left?" she asks, willing to change the subject once again.

I shake my head.

"Oh, Devyn. Please tell me you told them your plans?"

"It's not like they care. They gave me the choice. I know they fully expected me to choose college, and I tried it."

"They'll worry about you."

I shake my head again. I don't believe that at all. If they cared enough to worry, then they would've helped me find an alternative that worked for both of us. When I approached them weeks and weeks ago about a double major, business and fashion, they shot me down and told me they wouldn't pay for school if it had anything to do with fashion.

They weren't going to waste their money even though I seemed hell-bent on wasting my time.

"When do you head back to campus?"

"Tomorrow evening," she answers as she glides to a stop near the rundown gas station. "Can't you just make it two more months? I liked your plan of attending my school and lying about your major."

I threw that plan at her a couple weeks ago. I could lie and say I was going for pre-law like my dad wanted me to, but taking classes that would help in the fashion industry.

"They'd be checking up on me because I mentioned my double major."

I want to cry right now. I don't want to run away, but wishing for parents who actually gave a shit about me was even less likely.

"Why not just stay gone for a week or so, and then come back home? They'll be so glad you're back, they'll let you do whatever you want."

"I wish that were true, but I think they wanted me to choose this. Now they no longer have to pretend they give a shit."

My statement is only half-true. I can't recall the last time they gave a shit at all. Why does it even matter how I want to spend my life? It's not like they were ever really involved at all.

"I still think this is the wrong choice," she says, indicating the bus stop sign. "Look at that guy? He's creepy as hell."

I look across the parking lot toward the guy she's talking about. He does look a little creepy, but it's not enough to change my mind.

"I have to do this."

"What am I supposed to tell your parents when they call asking where you are?"

"They won't call," I assure her. "I left a note."

She shakes her head but doesn't ask what the note said. The friend who left for college a few months ago would have, but we've both changed in such a short period of time.

She has new friends, different obligations than I do. I can't be mad at her for that.

I unbuckle my seatbelt and reach across the console.

She wraps her arms around me. It feels like a more serious goodbye than I had originally intended.

"Call me if you need me," she whispers. Emotions clog my throat, leaving me incapable of words. I nod my head in agreement, but deep down I know that it probably won't happen. Other than a conversation, she's really not in any position to help me.

I have to help myself, even if that means taking a chance on life.

She releases me, opening her car door at the same time I do mine. My suitcase is already pulled out of her back seat before she can make her way around the back of the car.

"I love you," she says when I start to wheel my way toward the bus that's pulling up.

"Love you, too," I tell her, my pulse racing as I walk away.

I try to convince myself that it's excitement rather than fear making my heartbeat bang around in my ears.

The creepy guy is waiting to go inside, but turns his attention to me after the bus driver takes the handle of my suitcase to stow it under the bus.

"After you, gorgeous," the creep says, bending in the middle as if he's a chivalrous man.

The stench of alcohol hits me in the face, but I do my best not to cringe away from him. Offending him would probably piss him off and make him act in a way I won't like.

"Thank you," I say, avoiding eye contact with him.

He's close enough as I climb up the stairs that I feel the warmth of his body against my back.

I fight the urge to get off and run back to Quincy's car, but a quick glance over my shoulder tells me she didn't stick around long enough to watch me leave. The logical part of me knows there's no sense in her feeling afraid by sticking around, but it still hurts.

I stiffen my spine as I walk down the aisle.

"Looks like that back seat is free," the guy behind me says, a threat in his voice.

I drop down beside a middle-aged woman who's sitting halfway down the aisle, smiling at her as she looks my way.

The guy behind me grumbles a few cuss words as he passes.

"I think you made the right choice, hon," she says, patting me on my leg before resting her head against an inflated pillow pressed against the window.

I know I may be safe right now. I also know that I'm facing nearly twenty hours of travel to get to where I'm going, including more than a dozen stops and two bus changes.

I'm left thinking that Quincy was right as the bus pulls away from the gas station. I also know that getting to New Mexico is not even half of the risks I have to take in order to start living my own life the way I want to.

I close my eyes, doing my best to rest, but sleep doesn't come.

There are so many things still up in the air. Even though my trip to the Cerberus clubhouse is the first leg of my journey, it's far from the last. I'm just hoping that the man who was once my brother's best friend remembers who I am. It's not like he's shown his face in the eleven years since he got my brother killed.

6

LEGACY

"It's weird, right?"

"Not really," I say, lifting a bottle of water to my lips.

"He put that kid in danger," Stormy mutters, his opinion clear in his tone. "Twice."

"That is Sunshine and Bishop's business."

He grunts in disapproval.

Thankfully, he remains silent as Ryder, Sunshine's little boy, opens up his present from his dad.

"Superman, nice," Stormy praises.

The next gift the kid opens is a small stack of books. It's clear the type of young man Sunshine is raising when he thanks Bishop for the books even though he's not as interested in them as he is in the gift from his biological father.

Little Jamie, Hound's oldest son, grins when Ryder hands him a book with a blue truck on the front.

Stormy places his drink on a side table before stepping in front of me. "And for the other birthday boy."

I stare at the envelope in his hands. It's innocuous as most things go, but the glint in his eyes tells me what's inside is anything but.

"We said appropriate gifts only," Hound warns, clearly getting the same vibe.

A wave of whispers goes around the room. The light in the room glints off of the golden envelope as he shoves it into my hands. Clearly others are in the know right now, and it makes me feel even more apprehensive.

I take the envelope, figuring that making a bigger deal out of this right now would only make it worse. Pulling open the flap, I see the logo for Hale-ish, the Denver sex club some of the folks from the club like to go to occasionally.

I've heard rumors that Hound and his wife Gigi go there sometimes. That's why he must've said what he said.

My only saving grace when people stare at me expectantly is the additional gift card inside. I pull it out and hold it up.

"It's a gift card to that new steak place out on the highway," I say, displaying it while shoving the other envelope into the back pocket of my jeans.

I glare at Stormy, wanting to ring his fucking neck. But getting violent in front of the kids would be frowned upon.

"We ate there last week," Ryder says with a wide grin. "The nuggets are delicious."

I look to him, grateful that a lot of the attention is off of me.

I almost laugh when he looks from the book in little Jamie's lap and back at me. I can practically see the wheels turning in his head before he speaks.

"Do you like trucks?"

Laughter fills the room, my own cheeks tugging up into a smile.

I turn back to Stormy, seconds away from wrapping my hands around his throat for putting me on the spot, but then I freeze, the steakhouse gift card falling from my fingertips.

"Devyn?" I ask, feeling as if I'm seeing a ghost.

This past week leading up to my birthday has been a weird one for me. I know it has a lot to do with it being the first one I've celebrated since Vaughn's death where I wasn't still in the military. It's the first one celebrated as a member of Cerberus. The two of us were always supposed to end up here.

My recent trip down memory lane included finding Devyn on social media when the search for her parents didn't produce any results.

I wouldn't recognize the young lady standing in front of me otherwise.

I knew when I scrolled through her social media a couple days ago that she'd grown from the sad little girl I last saw at Vaughn's funeral into a beautiful young woman. I couldn't really consolidate the two of them.

Even now with her standing across the room, it's as if I conjured her from some dark place inside of me that needed some form of proof that it's okay to be happy with the life I've been allowed.

But maybe she's here for another reason. Maybe she's here for vengeance, a form of retaliation for her brother's death. It wouldn't be unheard of for a family to hyperfocus on revenge and to instill that same need for vengeance in their only living child.

"Emmett," she says, a hint of boredom in her tone. Her eyes scan up and down my body as if she's assessing me.

I shift on my feet, not liking her scrutiny at all.

"Who is that?" I nearly growl when I see the middle-aged man standing beside her.

She lifts her chin an inch or so higher before speaking. "That's the man who's going to marry us."

I almost huff a laugh but the seriousness in her tone prevents it. "Marry us?"

"Is she pregnant?" I hear Sunshine whisper. "She looks awful young."

My eyes immediately drop to her waist. Her stomach is flat under the dress she has no business wearing. I fight the urge to claw out Stormy's eyes since he's the only other single man in the room.

"Hi," my boss says as he steps forward with his hand out. "I'm Kincaid, and you are?"

"My best friend's little sister," I answer for her.

Gigi squeals, ever the one to like a messy situation. The woman thrives on drama, and I know it drives Hound fucking crazy.

Devyn ignores everyone in the room as she holds up a tattered little book. I know it's one of her journals. She always had one with her, doodling in them to pass the time.

"You told me that if you turned thirty and weren't married, you'd marry me. Happy birthday by the way."

My brows draw closer together. I remember no such damn promise. I'd fucking never. The girl was a damn baby when Vaughn and I had left for the Corps.

"That makes you what, eighteen now?" I ask.

"And three months," she says, the devious smile never leaving her face.

"You were a child when I made that promise."

"Dad?" Gigi says, speaking to Kincaid, the giddiness no longer in her tone.

The implication that's there makes my skin crawl.

"It wasn't like that," I mutter to everyone in the room.

"You promised Vaughn," she says, her smile and that self-confidence she had faltering a little.

Did she honestly expect to walk in here and get an agreement from me because of something written in a journal from over ten years ago? I'm a man of integrity, and I keep my word, but this is taking that a little too far.

"That's not fair," I tell her, my legs still locked in place, our conversation happening too far apart for it to be private.

I feel every eye in the room volleying back and forth as we work through this.

"I'm not going to marry you."

"Next!" Stormy says, stepping around me and giving Vaughn's little sister a seductive smile.

Thankfully, for his sake, she doesn't pay him any mind.

"Maybe we should take this to another room?" Kincaid says, offering me the reprieve I need right now.

"Will there be a wedding or not?" the man who accompanied Devyn here asks.

"No," I hiss just as Devyn says, "Yes."

She's out of her damned mind.

It'll never happen for so many reasons I'd be an old man if I had to stand here and list them all.

Kincaid frowns as he looks at the man. "There will not."

His voice is full of authority. I'm glad the man has gotten involved, but at the same time, these are my colleagues. Devyn being here is going to bring up so many questions about shit I never wanted to talk about outside of the therapy sessions with Dr. Alverez that Cerberus requires.

"Someone owes me five hundred dollars," the guy says, annoyance in his tone that his time has been wasted.

I don't miss a beat, pulling my wallet out and handing over the money to the man.

I feel Devyn's eyes drilling a hole into the side of my face, but I'll deal with her later.

"You signed it," she growls as the man folds the money and shoves it into his pocket so quickly, it makes me think he's afraid I'll change my mind and take it back from him.

Pages flutter close to my face as she turns the journal around for me to look at. I don't give a shit what that book says. She has to be clinically insane if she thinks I'll marry her because of something written in that damn book.

The man I just paid hasn't moved, and I watch, rage bubbling inside of me when I see him look back at Devyn, his eyes drifting down her body.

"Brent," Sunshine whispers, and I know she's caught on to the same thing I have.

This type of man has no fucking business even stepping foot on Cerberus property. It makes me wonder what he did to her before they arrived. It's been a long time since I had to take a life with my bare hands, but that clock is about to be reset.

"You coming with me?" he has the balls to ask, as if he isn't standing in the middle of a room full of fucking scary-ass men.

I can't even get my mouth open fast enough to answer for her when a resounding echo of noes fill the room.

Disappointment fills his eyes as he gives her one last once-over before turning around and walking toward the front door.

Hound and Shadow fall in line behind him. I know they won't let the man leave the property without explaining how unwelcome his return would be.

"The conference room," Kincaid says, his eyes on me.

"Devyn," I mutter, turning and indicating the room thirty feet away. "Let's talk in there."

She huffs like a spoiled brat and turns to go into the conference room.

Kincaid stops me, a hand raised before I can follow her.

"I swear to you," I begin, feeling the need to explain myself. "I would never hurt a child."

"She's no longer a child," he says. "But I saw the way you looked at her when she walked in."

I clench my jaw. I don't know how to respond to his observation.

He steps out of my way after a quick nod of his head.

The reminder that she's technically an adult at eighteen and three months doesn't matter. To me, she'll always be Vaughn's baby sister.

7

Devyn

My hands are trembling, and I'm too wound up to determine if it's from anger or nerves.

My confidence waned the second the preacher I found online pulled up in front of the clubhouse. Not only is the building bigger than I expected it to be, but the rows of cars and motorcycles outside told me that Emmett wasn't going to be the only one here.

All self-assurance drained away when I stepped inside and saw dozens of people. It's clear they were having a party, and honestly, I'm a little jealous that he has so many people willing to show up to celebrate his birthday. If it weren't for Quincy buying me a gift each year, I'd spend my own wallowing in self-pity. It's been years since my parents even bothered to mention that July twentieth was different from any other day of the year. The only consolation is that they don't celebrate their own birthdays either.

My eyes snap up at him when the door closes. I'm surprised that he's here alone. I was certain that Kincaid guy, clearly the big boss around here, was going to stick his nose where it doesn't belong.

I can't help the way my eyes roam over the way his t-shirt clings to the muscles in his chest. There isn't a single thing about him that's similar to the boys walking the halls of high school. I wouldn't be surprised if he pounded his fist against his chest and demanded that he's a man.

I considered him old when I searched for him online. I mean, thirty is like ancient, but Jesus, the man is smoking hot. I lick my lips, feeling my cheeks heat when I realize he probably can read every thought on my mind. I'm not exactly an expert at hiding my attraction to someone. Seb called me out on it months ago when he caught me drooling over him. If he hadn't, I never would've had the courage to flirt with him.

I've used the journal he signed as a means to get my foot in the door, but I have to acknowledge there's a real chance I could like this guy, as inappropriate as that might be. I knew he'd never fall for it. I'd question his sanity if he did. But I couldn't walk in here and be like *Hey, remember me? The little sister of the guy you let die in the Middle East*?

I scrunch my nose as the thought infiltrates my head. That's not something I'd ever say. Those are words from my mother's mouth, and I hate that she's in my head.

With his hands splayed, his palms open at his sides, he inches closer to me. It makes me feel as if the man sees me as some wounded animal.

"Did that man touch you in any way?" he asks, something akin to real concern in his tone.

"What?" I scrunch my nose again, the unfamiliar care confusing me. "The minister guy?"

"I doubt he was a real minister," Emmett mutters. "Did he hurt you?"

"No." I shake my head to drive my point a little further. "The guy wouldn't take his eyes off my legs on the drive over, but he didn't touch me."

Emmett's eyes drop to the hem of my dress, and it takes immense control not to shift on my feet with his attention on my bare skin. I really need to learn how to regulate my reactions better.

"Do your parents know where you are?"

I clench my jaw. Of course, he'd ask about them.

"I left them a note."

"A note?" The growl in his question shoots a wave of chill bumps up my spine. It only takes seconds before they're racing down my arms and legs.

"They kicked me out," I confess, automatically stopping him in his tracks.

"Are you pregnant?"

I jerk my head back. "Why the fuck would you ask me that?"

"Watch your mouth," he snaps.

"Why is that always the first damn question women get asked when they have a problem? No, I'm not pregnant. I didn't want to go to college. Leaving home was the only alternative they gave."

"The Malloys I knew would never kick their child out."

"They aren't the Malloys you knew," I hiss.

I've seen the pictures from my early childhood and the ones from Vaughn's life before. My parents were happy people. They smiled, and we took vacations. Emmett was in so many of them. He looked like the second Malloy son.

"But you wouldn't know that, would you?" I continue. "With Vaughn gone, you couldn't be bothered to ever come back to Broken Bow."

I don't actually know if he ever returned. I recall him from the funeral. Seeing him standing in the distance is a core memory of mine, but I know his family moved shortly after that. Seb's family now lives in his old house.

"School is important, Devyn," he says rather than giving any more attention to my accusation. "Vaughn wouldn't like you—"

"Don't," I snap. "You don't get to speak of him."

Pain flashes in his eyes, but he doesn't argue.

I instantly regret yelling at him. Vaughn was so important to so many people that he left a crater in many lives when he died, the biggest hole of all right in the very center of my house. My parents were never the same. My life changed that day. I didn't get the loving home that Vaughn grew up in. I was left with the shells of two loving parents, people who no longer had the ability to love. It's as if it drained out of them and seeped into the ground he was buried in.

I swallow against the guilt I feel. My memories of Vaughn are very few. His death happened so long ago that they seem more like stories told to me by someone else, as if the memories never belonged to me, but something I imagined as someone else spoke.

The same goes for Emmett. He and Vaughn were attached at the hip, closer than I imagine a set of twins would be.

"You need to go home," he says. "Running away isn't the answer."

"I didn't run away." My irritation with the man is growing by the minute. "You were a Marine. Marines are known for their honor, and I need you to honor your promise to me." I hold the ratty journal up.

He doesn't bother to look down at the damn thing.

"I expect you to follow through."

My mind races to the possibility of him actually doing it. Hell, I'd probably back out before it could happen, but what if it does? My gaze drops to his strong hands. The clench and release of his fingers make me think of them on my skin, garnering another wave of anxiousness and something I can only identify as anticipation.

"I will not marry you." He says the words slowly as if he thinks I'm having a hard time understanding. "For all you know, I could already be married."

I huff a humorless laugh. "If that were the case, I'd expect your wife would be in here with you. Besides, I checked your social media, and it says you're single."

"Because everything you find on the internet has to be true?"

My pulse pounds as I consider that I've made a huge mistake. The guy is smoking hot. It wouldn't be completely unreasonable that he's already been snatched up.

Embarrassment heats my cheeks as I search his eyes for answers before they drop to his left hand.

"No ring."

"Doesn't mean anything. Lots of men don't wear wedding rings."

"I think any woman who married you would require it. She'd want everyone to know you're off the market."

He shifts on his feet, looking a little uncomfortable.

"Vaughn would want—"

"Vaughn thought we were idiots every time we signed one of those pages in your journal. We wanted you out of our hair."

My chin trembles. The things I can recall from my childhood before Vaughn died was a smiling brother who involved me as much as he could given our age differences. Maybe those memories are something I created in my head, making that time with him seem perfect because I lost him. It wouldn't be the first time someone forgot all the bad in favor of the good. It happens every day.

I blink against the threat of tears. I was an idiot for coming here. If my parents don't care about me, if my best friend is too busy living her new life to even stick around long enough to watch the bus leave the parking lot, why did I ever think this man would give a shit?

"We probably had girls coming over and—"

I tear my eyes away from him, and he stops speaking, knowing he got his point across.

I know how I'd react if I had a younger sibling trying to get in my business and followed me around all the time, but being told you were seen as nothing more than an annoying brat still has a certain kind of sting to it.

I nod, unable to look him in the eyes.

"I'll leave."

He shifts to the side, blocking my path but making sure not to touch me as I try to walk past him.

"Where will you go?"

"Not really your concern, now is it?" I manage when all I really want to do is curl up into a ball and cry like a baby.

Independence is one thing. Being told no one wants you is a whole other ballgame. Even after living in a home with absentee parents, hearing that one more person in my life isn't interested in me is like a slap in the face. I think everyone wants to be wanted, and it's a jagged pill to swallow, knowing there isn't a soul on the earth who even cares.

Quincy hasn't called or texted, and I know it makes me petty to not have called or texted her either. Testing our friendship in this way isn't healthy on any level.

When I go to step around him again, his hand reaches for me, the warmth of it wrapping around the inner part of my elbow.

It's an inoffensive touch, one I wouldn't normally bat an eye at, but there's something different in it. Something that makes my heart race with more than the disappointment I felt mere seconds before.

I look from his hand on me to his green eyes before locking on his mouth.

How in the hell did I go from showing up here with no real plan, to wanting to kiss this man?

8

LEGACY

I know what I said to her was mean.

Hell, as truthful as those words were, I'm not looking down at Devyn Malloy right now and seeing a little girl.

Her height, the willfulness in her eyes, and the length of that damn dress she's wearing, don't allow me to see her as Vaughn's little sister.

I swear she's staring at my mouth. Instinctively, I lick my suddenly dry lips, watching as she subconsciously mimics the action.

I release her, taking an immediate step away.

There's no fucking way I'm attracted to her.

Granted, I can objectively look at a woman and see she's attractive, but internalizing any of that where she's concerned would be a mistake of epic proportions.

She's no longer a child.

I hate Kincaid's voice in my head right now.

Perfectly legal and morally right are two very fucking different things.

Knowing that still doesn't keep me from taking her in. It doesn't stop me from looking at her dark silky hair and wondering how it would feel flowing between my fingers. Her bright blue eyes are similar enough to Vaughn's that I have to look away.

No matter how pretty she is, I can never forget *who* she is.

"Are you going to let me stay?" she asks, even though she was seconds from walking out of the room less than a minute ago.

"I don't own this place, Devyn. I work here."

"You're not allowed guests?"

My throat works on a rough swallow at the implication my mind reads in her words.

"I can't just invite people to stay. There are rules."

"What are the rules?" she challenges.

Don't have random women over when events are planned with kids. Make sure the people you entertain are fully clothed when in the public areas unless otherwise planned. You know, basic MC shit, despite those parties I've heard so much about that haven't happened since I arrived.

Her eyes grow watery as I stand there, refusing to answer.

"I have nowhere else to go." She hangs her head, defeat tensing her shoulders.

I feel like a complete shithead right now, but maybe she wasn't lying.

I know the Katrina Malloy who called me a murderer and told me she hated me and never wanted to see me again was not the same woman who hugged me goodbye and told me to be safe the day Vaughn and I shipped off for basic training.

I guess it would be fitting that their grief bled into the relationship they had with their daughter. Even though I don't think I could neglect one child after the loss of another, people have their own way of dealing with their pain. I don't get to judge how anyone heals, especially when I was part of the reason they lost their child.

I wasn't joking when I told her that Vaughn wouldn't approve of her leaving home, but he'd be less impressed if I sent his little sister packing into an unsafe world. I mean, look at the trouble she found already in that man she had bring her here. If she left with him, at a minimum, he'd try to touch her. I shiver at how bad it could've been. I've seen how dangerous horny entitled men are. We fight against them all the time through our work with Cerberus. Just thinking of the man and the possibility of what he could've done to her makes me want to go find him and rip his fucking arms off.

That mental reaction tells me everything I need to know about what's going to happen here today. There's no way I'll send her out into the world alone. If she's being honest, there's no sense in taking her back home only for her to leave again because her parents won't let her stay.

"Stay right here," I snap, annoyed that my day now looks nothing like it did when I woke up this morning.

I turn and leave the room, pulling the conference room door closed behind me.

I'm not a man who really believes in manifesting things into reality, but there has to be some connection between Vaughn being on my mind a lot lately and his sister showing up at the clubhouse.

Kincaid and Emmalyn walk toward me the second I lock eyes with my boss.

Everyone's conversation halts as they look in my direction. I feel like I'm putting on a performance.

Luckily, Kincaid and his wife follow me a few feet further down the hallway so I don't have to have this conversation with a large audience. It won't stop people from whispering or from speaking about it in small groups.

The one bad thing about Cerberus is there are never really any secrets. We don't speak about our work to anyone other than those in Cerberus, but the folks in the club are like little old women gossiping every chance they get. This situation will be no different. I'm already pre-annoyed at the conversations I know I'm going to have.

"She can stay at our house," Emmalyn says before I can even open my mouth to explain what the full situation is.

I want to argue, but it's not like she wouldn't be safe there.

The only other alternatives would be her staying in my room or in one of the empty rooms in the clubhouse. The latter doesn't appeal to me at all considering Stormy's eagerness to step forward and joke about marrying her. The former, staying in my room, makes me feel shit I have no business allowing to creep into my head.

"I would really appreciate that," I say.

"That guy?" Em asks, her hand coming up to her throat.

"She says he didn't hurt her," I assure them, praying Devyn was being honest with me. "I'll let her know about staying with you guys."

I walk away from them, wondering if I'll ever not get pissed when thinking about the man who accompanied her here. My wager on that is it'll never happen.

I walk back into the conference room, leaving the door open this time. If she's going to be around here for any period of time, she might as well get used to people being in her business.

"Kincaid, my boss, and his wife, Emmalyn, said you can stay with them."

Her face falls as if she's disappointed that I've helped find her a place to stay. I swear this generation of ungrateful—

"I thought I'd be staying with you."

"Abso-fucking-lutely not," I snap.

"I figured we need to get to know each other better before the wedding."

I step in closer to her.

"There will be no fucking wedding, Devyn. You need to—"

When laughter bubbles out of her throat, I realize she was joking. The playful glint in her eyes is worlds better than the tears that were there earlier. It also tells me that she never expected me to fall for that promise I made all those years ago.

I'm questioning my sanity when a small wave of disappointment hits me as I follow her out of the room.

9

Devyn

"You met Kincaid," Emmett says as he walks up to the guy he claims is his boss. "This is his wife, Emmalyn."

I shake her hand when she holds it out to me. She has a kind smile, the type that you can tell she uses often, the evidence in the shallow wrinkles around her eyes and mouth.

"Please call me Em. It's lovely to meet you, Devyn. We have a room at our house we'd love for you to stay in if you'd like."

I almost turn her down. The kindness doesn't seem like it's forced, but it's not something I'm used to.

Quincy's moms are lovely women. They treat me well, but it took me a long time to get used to them showing any concern over me. This woman knows nothing about me and is already looking at me like she cares. Although it doesn't seem fake, how could it possibly be real? I understand compassion. I see it in online videos all the time of people taking in stray animals and nurturing them back to health, but I'm not a damned dog.

I give her the best smile I can manage.

"I'd really appreciate that," I say, because even though I'm not exactly comfortable with it, I wasn't lying when I told Emmett I have no other options. Besides, it's not like I plan on staying here forever. Maybe the jobs in New Mexico pay better than the one I had in Nebraska. It might be possible for me to make enough money to get out on my own faster than I did back home.

I look to my left, needing reassurance from the only person in the room that I know—even though I can't really say I know Emmett—only to find him gone. The man couldn't get away from me fast enough.

I have no doubt he sees me as the brat he claimed Vaughn saw me as all those years ago. I smile again at Emmalyn.

"Let me show you around," she says before lifting on her toes and pressing her lips to Kincaid's cheek.

The man looks hard. I'd make the assumption that he was a criminal if I ran into him on the street. I would still think that way if it weren't for the way his eyes soften when he looks down at his wife. I don't know that I've ever seen that level of love on someone's face. The unfamiliar sight of it makes me feel like I'm intruding on a special moment, so I look away from them.

"I can show you the daycare," she says as she steps up beside me, sweeping her arm back in the direction of the conference room.

"I don't know what Emmett told you, but I'm not pregnant."

She chuckles, the tinkling sound calming rather than making me feel as if she's somehow mocking me.

"I didn't assume you were. We don't mind you staying but everyone earns their keep around here."

Em pulls open the door to one room, only to have to use a key to unlock the interior half door.

The room is very organized with a diaper changing area, a crib area, and several little stations meant for play. The toys range from playmats for infants to larger toys for older children.

"I'm not really good with kids," I confess, wondering what else I could do to earn my keep.

My mind races back to walking into this place and how many men there were in the room.

I'm not one to stereotype, but if she suggests earning my keep on my back, I'll be out the door so damn fast, people will wonder if there was a fire with how hot my shoes heat up.

"We can find something else for you, but our daycare isn't chaotic. Only kids belonging to club members are allowed. Well, also club members' grandkids."

"Grandkids?" I didn't see a guy out there old enough to have grandkids.

"Diego and I have five grandkids."

I do my best to keep the look of shock off my face. I'd mean it as a compliment but I don't know if she'd read it that way if I told her she looks great for having five grandkids. I opt to keep my mouth shut. I'd be a fool to even risk upsetting someone so willing to help me.

"We have several people that work here, but we could always use more help. The Cerberus family has been growing by leaps and bounds."

I nod in understanding. "I'm not good with kids."

It's a repeat of my earlier words, and I know she heard me.

"I'm not trying to be disrespectful," I rush out, not wanting to make her mad. "I just have very limited experience and babies kind of scare me."

She chuckles, no sounds of irritation in her laughter.

"You wouldn't be the first, but if you'd prefer to help out in other ways, there's always something to do around here."

"I could work outside of the clubhouse. I worked at a retail store back home. Do they have any Lucky Dollar stores here?"

I loathed that job, but it wasn't hard work. I can't exactly be picky about what I do.

"There aren't," she says.

"I could work anywhere and pay rent."

She could easily charge whatever she wanted, and I wouldn't be able to argue. Maybe the daycare wouldn't be so bad, I think as I look back at the changing table. I do my best not to shudder.

"We don't need money. We need physical help, and we don't hire from outside of the club. We're very strict about who we allow onto the property. It's why so many people were on edge with that creepy guy here."

"He was creepy," I quickly agree, refusing to consider what could've happened to me.

After the trip here from Nebraska, it's easy to see now how so many people end up missing or in sketchy situations.

"We have a luncheon for the local women's shelter coming up. You could help with that. We also have a couple new guys arriving soon, and their rooms will need a quick once-over."

"I could help with all of that," I tell her with a genuine smile.

"Perfect," Em says as we walk out of the room.

I'm not going to complain, but I don't understand their kindness and quickness to help a complete stranger. I fully expected to show up and have to fight tooth and nail in order to even be allowed to stay a single night, but the man my parents made Emmett seem isn't panning out from what I've seen so far today.

"Did you have belongings?"

"Yes, ma'am. I left them on the front porch." I drop my eyes and kick my toe against a spot on the floor. "I didn't know if I'd be allowed to stay."

"Let's go get them," Em says. "It's a scary world out there, and we never send someone away who needs help."

I may not know the woman but I do believe she's being completely honest.

Emmett is standing off to the side, speaking with one of the other guys, but I dart my eyes away a second after spotting him. I have no real connection to the man, so there's no point in trying to be his friend or anything.

Kincaid, or Diego as Em calls him, falls in line with us out the front door. He frowns when the weight of the suitcase is much heavier than it seems he expected.

"Did you pack rocks?" he asks, a wry grin on his face.

"Just the essentials." My packing choices now make me feel immature. "I didn't have much room for anything else after I got my sewing machine in there."

"I can get it," Emmett says, holding out his hand to his boss. "Dominic was looking for you."

Kincaid nods, handing the suitcase over.

He doesn't say a word as we walk back through the building and out the back door. I noticed the pretty houses across the street but the house Em is directing us to appears a little older than those, but no less impressive.

"There's a pool?" I ask, feeling younger than I am with the urge to run and cannonball into it, despite it being fall.

"We have two," Em says, pointing to a building to the right. "One is indoors."

The cleanliness and landscaping makes it look and feel like a well-maintained resort.

I look over to Emmett, but his face is impassive. It makes me wonder about his travels in the military. Has he seen so many amazing things that he takes all of this for granted? Has he been here so long that he no longer sees it as impressive?

My parents provided a comfortable life for me, but we didn't have two pools. There wasn't a massive swing set and jungle gym worthy of a country club in our backyard like they have for the kids here.

"That's Misty's house," Em says, pointing down another sidewalk. "And over there is where Khloe lives. Rob and Jaxon live over there."

I catch myself watching Emmett rather than looking in the direction of her pointing finger. He keeps his eyes locked ahead, his back stiff as if he's forcing himself to act in a certain way.

He waits at the bottom of the stairs for Em and me to climb up, and suddenly I feel self-conscious that he's directly behind me. Are his eyes on my legs or is it the heat from the sun?

"It's the spare bedroom up the stairs, directly to the left," Em explains.

I stand there awkwardly, and Emmett does the same until I make a move in that direction.

He follows, lifting the suitcase and placing it on the bed without a word. Before I can think of some form of small talk, he's gone, leaving me standing there alone. The dismissive behavior is familiar. What's new is the burn of unshed tears behind my eyes because of the sadness it brings.

I know I shouldn't expect more from him, but it didn't stop hope from blooming in my chest when he didn't grab me by the arm and toss me out the front door.

I'll have to take everyone's kindness, because there's nothing else for me right now. But I also have to keep in mind that it won't last. Eventually the charity will wear off, and I'll be given another ultimatum. I guess I'll just have to do my best around here to prolong it as long as I can.

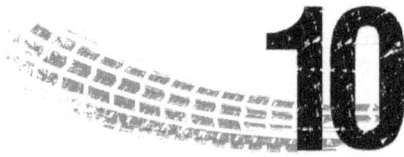

10

LEGACY

I hate the visceral reaction I have to her when I walk into the clubhouse kitchen the next morning to find her standing at the sink, her hands covered in soap suds from washing dishes.

A chuckle jerks my head to the left. Not for the first time in the last twenty-four hours, I want to strangle Stormy. The wide grin spreading across his face tells me that he saw every second of my reaction, but I feel better knowing he's watching me and not her.

I look around, assessing who else is in there, before lifting my hand and shooting him a middle finger. It only makes him laugh harder, drawing Devyn's attention.

It shouldn't seem like a seductive tease when she glances over her shoulder, making a lock of her damn hair stick to her cheek. She blows at it twice before giving up when it doesn't move.

"Good morning," she says, her eyes assessing me as if she thinks I'm going to have unkind words for her.

"Morning," I mutter, shifting my eyes to the coffee pot because keeping them on her wouldn't be a smart move.

I need to think of anything else than the things I've thought where Devyn Malloy is concerned since she showed up yesterday. The sight of her has shifted things though because her hair is wet, clearly from a shower, but she's still wearing the same dress from yesterday.

It makes me wonder what the hell she had packed in that heavy suitcase if not clothes to change into.

I pour myself a cup of coffee, forgoing the sugar because the bowl on the counter is empty, and I'd have to walk past her again to get the bag from the cabinet.

"Sleep well?" Stormy asks, his voice full of laughter as I sit down at the table beside him.

I could've easily sat across from him, putting my back to her, but I'm obviously not as capable of doing the right thing as I thought I was.

I consider that maybe she lied about being kicked out. If she packed in a hurry, that would be more believable, meaning there's a real possibility she ran away. I considered all of this last night, but I still didn't pick up the phone and call her parents. She's young, but technically an adult, so I guess she can't actually run away. She was insistent that the parents I knew the Malloys to be and the people they are now aren't the same, but I'm having a hard time consolidating those two things. Death, however, has a way of changing people. Vaughn's changed me, so it's not much of a stretch to consider his parents changed too.

"What are—"

"Don't fucking start with me," I warn under my breath.

Thankfully, the man doesn't open his mouth again. Before long, Em, Misty, and Khloe are all in the kitchen.

"Stormy, there's another box of supplies on the back porch," Em says. "Can you grab them for me?"

"Yes, ma'am." He's up and out of the kitchen in a flash.

I take the opportunity to stand from the table, taking my cup with me. I'll bring it back later and wash it myself, if only to avoid any interaction with Devyn.

I haven't decided how I feel about her being here. I don't begrudge the girl a safe place to land for a while, but her presence is interfering with my head. I don't like that part of it.

"Hey," Em says, following me out of the room.

I fight the urge to grow instantly defensive. I know how the situation looks—a young girl showing up at the clubhouse demanding I marry her. I know Em noticed that she's wearing the same clothes as yesterday.

"I was hoping you could take her shopping," Em says. "She brought a sewing machine in her suitcase rather than clothes."

My frown matches Em's. It proves just how damn immature Devyn is, as if some form of crafting is more important than necessities.

"I'd offer to take her, but I get the feeling she'd tell me no. Since you know her—"

"I don't know her," I assure Em. "I was friends with her brother. I haven't seen that girl since... it's been a really long time. She was a child, but I didn't—"

I snap my mouth closed when Em holds her hand up. I have a million things to say, but I'd never cross a line and do anything that would look disrespectful to Kincaid's wife.

"No one thinks anything untoward happened between you and her, Legacy, so get that out of your head. As old as the connection is between the two of you, it's still a stronger one than any of us have. She's skittish and suspicious of every move Diego and I have made since she arrived yesterday. I think she'd feel more comfortable with you."

I nod. It makes sense. If she's been living with parents who made her choose between college and leaving home, I guess there's a real chance she hasn't been shown much compassion in her life.

"Did she say how long she was staying?"

Em shakes her head.

"Did she say anything about still thinking I'm going to marry her?"

Em shakes her head again.

I blow out a breath of relief.

"She's been quiet, reserved. Grateful for the help we've offered. I haven't pressed her for information. Maybe you can get more out of her on the drive into town."

I don't argue with the woman as she pats my arm in a motherly way. Half of me wants to ask Devyn a million questions, but the other half is left wishing she never came to the clubhouse. Although there isn't a day that goes by that Vaughn doesn't cross my mind, seeing his little sister here is too much. I know he'd want her safe at home with their parents.

I pull my phone from my pocket, but I just can't seem to bring myself to make the call.

I don't blame the Malloys for their hatred toward me. It's not anything I haven't felt for myself, but placing that call seems like a betrayal. If Devyn wanted to let her parents know where she was, she could easily provide that information herself.

It's not greater than the pain of losing Vaughn, but the day his mother told me she hated me and never wanted to see me again, I lost more than him. They were my family, too. Mrs. Malloy always treated me like her own child. My parents were the same way with Vaughn. There was always two of everything for both of us—two Christmases, two Easter baskets.

My parents grieved as if they lost a child as well when they got the news. In a way, they did. They loved him unconditionally. They were shunned too. The pain in the Malloys' eyes each time they'd see each other was so painful that they moved less than a year after Vaughn died.

I sneak another peek into the kitchen on my way to my bedroom. I realize halfway down the old hallway that I've been moved to the newer part of the clubhouse rather than the old. Muscle memory is a bitch, but I can say there isn't a single part of me that has wanted to ruffle Devyn's hair like I did a million times when she was a child. Tangling my fingers in the dark curls, however...

11

Devyn

I haven't always been the best at reading people. Well, actually, I've tried and made mistakes. I attribute that to having parents who I think love me, but I don't recall the last time they actually said it. I mean, they kept a roof over my head growing up, but they were also absent a lot. There but not really there, if that makes sense.

So the twitch of Emmett's jaw and the way he's gripping the steering wheel until his knuckles turn white is hard for me to read. Is he mad? Annoyed? Wishing he were anywhere but here in the SUV with me?

I could easily ask, but he hasn't said a word past asking me if I was ready to head to the women's shelter.

What I do know is that the food dishes that we put in the back could've easily fit in the SUV with Em and Misty, but they were adamant that the food go in this one and that I ride with him. I didn't get the vibe that they were annoyed with me, but as previously stated, I'm not the best at reading people.

I sigh, drawing in a deep breath and releasing it in a rush. The world would be a lot calmer, more welcoming, if people just said what they needed to say and moved past it, rather than bottling all that mess up inside of them. If he's annoyed with me, then tell me. It's not like I have any control over this situation right now. Hell, I don't have control over a single thing in my life other than what time I go to bed. With Em and Diego turning in so early, it felt disrespectful to stay up and make noises that could bother them. So, I guess, I don't even control that these days.

He doesn't make a noise or ask me why I'm annoyed. It's all too familiar, the exact way my parents acted while I was growing up when I tried to engage them without having to speak first.

I pull out my cell phone, wondering how long I'll get to keep it because my parents pay the bill. I'm certain they won't continue to pay for it with me gone.

Pulling up local social media groups, I swipe through them, looking for people who need help with any form of sewing project. I've made decent money in the past filling orders for people, and I figure since I'm not working outside of the clubhouse, this would be a great way to start saving some cash.

I torture myself with reading listings I know I can't help with. My sewing machine isn't the right tool for embroidery, which seem to be the overwhelming majority of requests.

I swipe through the images one poster made about personalized footballs, switching to a crafting app that has step-by-step instructions on how to do exactly that even though I know it's not something I could do. The guy is looking for someone to do all of this for his entire league, citing that it would be over a hundred balls. It's a lot of work, something that would be a major undertaking even if I had the right equipment.

I consider selling my regular sewing machine with the hopes that I could find an embroidery machine with enough power to complete the order, but deep down I know the order would be snatched up before I could get all of those ducks in a row. The crafting app also explains overhead costs and gives a great calculator for what the suggested charge should be for each individual item as well as pricing for bulk orders. The profit alone makes me wish I could make it happen.

As the SUV slows to a stop, I'm looking online for gently used machines and coming up empty. I regret being responsible and not getting a credit card when Quincy told me about the one she got for emergencies while she was going to be on campus for college. I could buy a new machine with the profit from the order, but it would require them paying in full before getting started. Even in my head that sounds like a scam, and something unlikely the requester would go for.

I close out of all the tabs on my phone, knowing any more research would be a further waste of time.

Embroidery on footballs, or even on the baseballs I saw some crafters doing, isn't what I want to do with my life, but at least it's sewing adjacent. Beggars can't be choosers and all that. I knew when I left home, I wouldn't just have my dream job land in my lap, but getting rid of my sewing machine seems like a step backward, not forward.

"Why are you making all those noises?" Emmett asks.

I lift my gaze to him, scrunching my nose at him in annoyance. Can't he see I'm in the middle of a life crisis?

I frown when I realize how dramatic that sounds even in my head.

"What's gotten you suddenly so annoyed?"

Ignoring his inciting questions, I try and shift the topic. "What do you think the chances are that I could get a loan?"

He shrugs. "I guess it depends on what you need it for. If you need money—"

"A business loan," I clarify. "From a bank."

His cheek twitches. "Slim."

His eyes drop to my mouth when I frown, and it has the power to derail every other thought in my head. I look away.

"I mean, you're young and interest rates are incredibly high right now. You have no job, no way to pay them back. You—"

"I fucking get it," I snap, unable to sit here and listen to my failures as an adult being ticked off on his fingers.

"And that mouth of yours is going to get you into trouble."

I shift in the seat and turn back to look at him. "As you stated, I may be young, but I'm an adult. I can speak however I like."

He doesn't look impressed with my declaration, but he also doesn't argue with it.

I attempt the mature thing and shift back to facing forward, but his eyes lock on the skin exposed on my legs. I have to fight the urge to climb in his lap when his tongue skates out, tasting the curve of his bottom lip. I may not be an expert at reading people, but there's no mistaking his attraction to me right now.

Instead of hating it because I feel like he insulted me, I say nothing, liking his attention on me.

I roll my lips between my teeth, fighting a smile when someone behind us honks. It makes him jerk his eyes back to the road, the light having turned green while he was focused on me.

I know I came to New Mexico and told him he promised to marry me all those years ago, but I also knew it would never happen. The notion of it is crazy. Our age difference is insane, more an issue for him I imagine that it would be for me, but still. Him watching me the way he just was doesn't gross me out at all. I felt the heat of his eyes in places I have no business imagining him seeing.

I lick my suddenly dry lips, my eyes glued out the window. I want to tease him about what just happened, in an effort to regain the upper hand, but I get the feeling it would have an adverse reaction. What I saw in his eyes was unfiltered, and the last thing I want is him thinking too hard when he looks at me.

"This is it?" I ask ten minutes later when he pulls into the parking lot of a non-descript building.

"It's a women's shelter," he explains. "It wouldn't be smart to advertise what it is."

"Sort of like houses involved with the underground railroad?"

He nods, his eyes locked on the front door. "Most of the agencies in town, like the hospitals, clinics, and churches, know this place exists, so they're able to refer women here when they reach out for help."

"Makes sense," I say, hating that places like this need to exist.

He climbs out, heading to the back of the SUV, and I follow suit.

"You may have to make more than one trip," he says, reaching in for the first casserole dish.

"Multiple trips?"

He waits for me to adjust the strap of my purse before placing the dish in my outstretched hands.

"Men don't go inside," he explains. "We're a trigger for some of the women."

That news makes this whole thing even sadder.

"It's their safe place," he continues. "We don't invade it."

I nod, swallowing down a lump threatening to form as I look up at him. I knew Emmett was a nice guy. Although my memories of him are few and more than a little faded by time, I can't recall a single moment when he was rude to me or told me to go find something else to do. Those memories are the same for Vaughn. If he was annoyed with me, it never registered.

"I'll be right back," I tell him, turning to go to the front door.

I'm wondering how I'll get the door open as I close the distance, but it pulls inward just as I step onto the concrete sidewalk running in front of it.

"Thank you," I tell the woman standing behind the door as I enter.

"Is there more?" she asks.

"Yes, but I'll grab them. If you want to take this one that would be great."

She holds her hands out, allowing me to shift the dish.

"I'll be right back. I'm Devyn by the way."

She nods, not giving me her name in return. I can only imagine that she's either extremely timid or she's nervous about disclosing who she is. I realize as I walk back to the SUV for the next dish that I can't really be upset with someone protecting themselves after going through hell.

"They're healing," Emmett says, reading the sadness in my eyes as I approach him. "That looks different for each one."

I nod, fighting tears, because, honestly, I can't imagine facing the world without my chin held high no matter what's in front of me. I consider the privilege I've been given in my life. It may not be perfect, but I never walked into my home afraid I'd be hit or abused.

"I'll wait out here for you," he says as he hands me the final dish.

I nod, knowing I can't speak right now because of the emotions threatening to bubble up.

The door opens once again, this time by a different woman. She has a smile on her face as I step inside.

"Is it lunch or dessert?" she asks, her eyes locked on the dish. "I would kill for anything with spiced apples in it right now."

"It's lasagna," I tell her, chuckling when her face falls. "But Em and Misty brought peach cobbler."

Her eyes widen. "Em's cobbler?"

I nod, feeling a little better about this place with her excitement.

"Is it good?"

"The best," she declares. "Follow me to the kitchen. The sooner we eat lunch, the sooner we can get to dessert."

"You can have dessert first if you want," Em tells her as we enter the large, commercial-grade kitchen.

The woman eyes the dishes set off to the right as if she's going to accept Em's offer, but she shakes her head with a chuckle.

"I can wait. It'll only make it that much better." She turns back in my direction. "I'm Sharron."

"Devyn," I tell her, letting her take the dish from my hands to add it to the line of dishes on the counter.

For the next fifteen minutes, Sharron and I help set the table and make sure there's enough ice for drinks. We're told that it's going to be a buffet-style lunch. Misty, the wife of Cerberus vice president Shadow, explains in a whisper that some will eat later while others may make a plate and go back to their rooms.

Giggles fill the air, making me realize this isn't a place for only women but their children as well. My heart seizes a little tighter as a couple kids run through the kitchen. I smile as I watch them, grateful that I'm not seeing faces with bruises, which is what I expected when Emmett told me what this place was.

One little girl runs past with a squeal of happiness as she's being chased by a little boy. They dart through and then move to the dining room. I grin as I watch them play, but then the little girl cuts a corner around one of the chairs too close and snags the strap of her pretty dress.

She stops running, the little boy ramming into her on accident. Tears immediately fill her eyes as they dart around. It's clear to see she's scared, as if she thinks she's going to be in trouble.

"It's fine," Em says, stepping forward just as the first bubble of a sob escapes the little girl's throat.

"It's ruined," she says through her tears. "I shouldn't have been running."

"You were playing, Millie," Em says as she crouches low to get on the little girl's level. "You're allowed to play."

She nods, her eyes wet with tears.

"It's not ruined," I say, stepping closer to her and reaching into my purse. "If it's okay with you, I can fix it right now."

Her eyes widen before darting to Em to make sure it's okay. I understand her need to verify she's safe, but it also makes me sadder that she's learned in her very short life that she can't trust everyone.

I hold up the sewing kit I always carry with me. "I think I even have a pretty pink color thread that will match it perfectly."

"I don't have anything to pay you with," she says, a hint of fear in her voice. I want to kill whatever person who told her she'd have to pay in some form in order to be worthy of help.

"I don't charge for minor repairs on Sundays," I explain.

She checks with Em one last time before stepping forward. "Don't poke me with the needle."

"I wouldn't dream of it," I say, pulling the pink thread out along with a needle. "Keep your hand right there."

I point to her chest so she'll be able to maintain her modesty.

She jerks away from me when I get closer with the needle.

"How about this?" I say, backing away and grabbing one of the small paper plates I put out by the dessert trays. "Hold it just inside your dress. That way the needle won't even have a chance to touch you."

She situates the plate under the edge of her dress, and smiles as I fix the strap, giving it a few extra stitches in case of another mishap while she's playing.

"Are you a fairy godmother?" Millie asks when I step back and she sees her dress is like new.

"No, but I'm always prepared for a fashion emergency." I hold up my sewing kit once again, smiling when she does.

"Thank you," she says before turning around and calling after the little boy she was playing with earlier.

"You said you weren't good with kids," Em says, a motherly smile on her face.

"I'm not. I'm good with clothes and sewing."

"You replaced her tears with a smile. That's being good with kids."

I want to talk to her about the loan like I did with Emmett, hoping to get a more educated response, but I know now isn't the time.

"After the luncheon, Legacy is going to take you shopping for some clothes," Em says. Her tone doesn't leave much room for argument.

Spending more time with him, especially if he's going to look at me the way I caught him looking at my legs, isn't such a bad thing. The way he made me feel is something I think I could easily grow addicted to.

12

LEGACY

I hate the way I stared at the front of the shelter, my eyes focusing on the windows each time a shadow passed in front of them. I felt like a creep, like a stalker of one of the women inside, as I waited for the lunch to end and for Devyn to come back outside.

I almost left to just drive around the block, but I was afraid she'd step outside and I wouldn't be there. As much as I don't want to be involved in the physical shopping, I don't want anyone else to take her either.

God, if she buys more dresses like the one she's wearing today, I may have to vocalize my opinion. What kind of asshole does that make me, thinking I have any kind of right to dictate what a woman wears?

I lift my chin as the front door opens, settling on the decision that I'll just knock the lights out of every guy who looks at her in a certain way, knowing I'll probably have to start with Stormy's ass first.

The fabric of that sinful dress swirls in the breeze, teasing me with the idea that it might lift high enough to see her...

I shake my head, doing my best to shove thoughts like that away.

I turn my eyes forward as she opens the passenger side door. It hits me that instead of gawking at her, I probably should've climbed out and opened the damn door for her.

Instead of saying a word, she busies herself with switching the Bluetooth over to her phone, pulling up a map that immediately instructs me to turn right out of the parking lot.

I tilt my head, mildly annoyed, but realize just as quickly that I can't exactly expect her to act the way I think she should. Which, honestly, is a jumble of half-illicit situations in my head I have no business thinking.

"Em says you're taking me shopping," she says, pointing to the map on the screen when I don't shift the SUV into drive. "This is where I'd like to go. They're one of the few places in town open today."

I nod, grateful I'm not going to have to argue with her like I thought I might have to.

The area of town grows less and less desirable with each block I drive. I'm less than impressed with where we end up when the map declares I've entered the parking lot for my destination.

"Really?" I ask, incapable of hiding the derision in my voice.

"Don't be a snob," she says, excitement lacing her tone.

"It's a thrift store," I say, as if she doesn't know where she was going to end up even though she typed the address into the map. "You don't have to buy clothes from here. You can pick anywhere."

"I figured no one would complain when I wasn't really given a choice about going shopping. Honestly, Emmett, this is where I'd go even if I weren't a charity case."

"You're not... Let's go." I'm not going to argue with her, but I wait for her to open her door before reaching into the glove box and pulling out a handgun.

"Is that really necessary?"

"Better safe than sorry," I mutter, sounding more like my dad than I like.

She shrugs, climbing the rest of the way out of the SUV. She waits near the hood while I conceal the weapon and join her.

Out of instinct, I press my hand to her lower back, refusing to look down at her when she tilts her head up at me. I also refuse to consider just how perfectly she tucks into my side. I have no business considering a damn thing where this woman is concerned.

"Are you scared?" she teases as I place myself between her and a guy sitting on the curb near the entrance. "You're acting like a bodyguard."

"You're the one that chose this part of town," I mutter, pulling the door open with my free arm, torn between walking inside ahead of her like I should to assess the danger, and sticking to her back so the guy on the curb can't get to her.

I opt to put myself between her and the known danger, letting her walk ahead of me. I run into her back when she pauses just inside the door so she can look around the store.

She has a smile on her face, her eyes wide like she's stepping into an amusement park rather than a place that smells musty and is cluttered with the things every other sane person has discarded from their lives.

Before she can tip over from me running into her, I reach my arm around her, preventing her from falling. Instead of stepping away, she turns her face up toward me, looking a little over her shoulder. I feel like an asshole when my fingers flex against her lower belly before I take a step back.

"You're sure you can find something here?" I ask, ripping my eyes away from her to scan the disorderly store.

"I know I'll find more than I could ever need," she says rather than challenging me about what just happened.

I wave my arm out in front of me, indicating that she should get to work.

At second glance, I see signs hanging from the ceiling, indicating where certain things are. I don't hover when she heads toward the section labeled WOMEN'S CLOTHING, but I also don't allow much distance between the two of us.

I'm not a snob. I don't have an issue with people buying things secondhand, but this part of town isn't exactly known as being a safe area. I'm well aware that crime can happen anywhere, but this part of Farmington has a reputation.

I stay at the end of each aisle that she goes in, all the while wondering if she even has a clue what she should do if someone came through the front door brandishing a weapon. I seriously doubt she's been given any formal training, but with the nature of the world these days, I also have no doubt she went through active shooter drills in high school, as fucked up as that is.

When she starts to look burdened by the clothes in her arms, I head to the front, nodding a hello at the woman sitting behind the counter looking bored as I grab a shopping cart for her.

I can't see anyone else in the store, but there are some shelving units in the far back corner that could be hiding other employees or patrons. The lack of witnesses makes the bump and rattle of the decrepit cart no less embarrassing as I push it closer to her.

She thanks me as I slide the cart toward her, placing the growing pile of clothes inside.

"That's a men's shirt," I say, pointing at the striped button-down on top before looking around again. "This is the men's section."

"You didn't seem like the type of guy that had hardened views on gendered clothing until just now. Then again, the way you looked at my dress earlier—"

"Get whatever you want," I say before she can vocalize her thoughts any further.

I knew she was too astute to miss the way my eyes dropped to her thighs in the truck earlier.

I try to distract myself with anything else, but of course she draws all my attention. I pull my eyes from her long enough to follow the shadow of the man out front as he stands up and starts to head away from the front door, but a second later, I'm looking at her again.

She pulls another men's shirt against her body, the damn thing so big she can almost wrap it all the way around her with it still buttoned in the front.

"That's too big," I say, analyzing my tone, thinking it sounds too damn fatherly. I cringe, imagining her seeing me that way.

Jesus, how disgusting am I? I feel like a creepy old man.

"Everything has to be altered," she says, not bothering to look in my direction. "The more fabric the better."

"Is this everything?" I ask a few minutes later when she leaves the racks of clothing.

She shakes her head, and somehow I'm left pushing the nearly full cart behind her as she heads to the section labeled *CRAFTS.*

As if she's looking for a treasure, Devyn sifts through every overflowing bin, pulling out buttons and things that could maybe be used as trim, now that I know she's planning to do some form of alterations on these clothes. She finds several spools of thread, putting back the ones that don't pass her test of tugging on it to make sure it doesn't break.

"That's only a dollar," I say when she tosses a lime green spool back that matches one of the items in the cart.

"It's too old. It does me no good if it breaks when I try to use it," she explains, her eyes lighting up when she holds up a pack of oversized sunflower buttons.

She tosses them in the cart before going back to digging through the next bin.

Her focus somehow makes her seem older. I haven't had much involvement with the younger crowd, other than new boot Marines joining the Corps, but even those guys would act immature often. She's showing such care and attention to her task, that it's unexpected.

I have to consider that this is just my brain trying to reason with me after the way I looked at her earlier.

Her age honestly doesn't matter because, at the end of the day, she's still Vaughn's younger sister, and completely fucking off-limits.

"And I think that's it," she says, dropping one final spool of thread into the cart.

I push the cart to the front register, helping her pull all the musty clothes, buttons, trimming, and thread from the cart and piling it on the counter.

I wave her away when Devyn reaches into her purse as if she's going to pay for the items. She nods, not arguing with me like I thought she was going to.

"Seventy-eight, forty-three," the woman says, treating the items with even less care than Devyn did as she placed them in the cart.

I pull cash from my wallet, unwilling to put a card into the janky reader.

I take my change, shoving it into my pocket so I can help Devyn with the bags. She thanks the cashier excitedly, wishing her a good day before turning toward the front exit.

"I thought it was going to be more than that," I say absently.

"They have really great prices. I can't wait to come back again."

I take a deep breath, fighting the urge to insist that she never come alone, unsure if it would sound protective or fatherly.

13

Devyn

I feel like a giddy girl imagining Harry Styles directly singing to her during a sold-out concert. He pressed his hand to my back not once but twice! I've never had a guy touch me like that. I felt safe and turned on all at the same time. It was an instant connection. As he climbs in behind the wheel, I find myself hoping for him to do it over and over.

I keep my eyes locked outside my window as he drives.

"Are you hungry?"

I almost answer with all the things I'm dying to taste, but no matter how he looked at me earlier, I doubt he'd ever give in to that part of him.

"I ate at the luncheon, but feel free to stop if you are."

He shakes his head. "I'll grab something back at the clubhouse."

It feels like it takes years to get back to Cerberus property, and I know that's because of how excited I am to get started on the clothes bagged in the back of the SUV. I could picture in my head exactly how I would change each one to make it my own style.

I climb out the second he places the vehicle in park outside the clubhouse, hurrying to the back to grab my bags. With his longer legs, Emmett is quicker, but he doesn't say a word when I eagerly snatch a bag from his hand.

Instead of just letting me go, he redirects me around to the right side of the building, keeping pace with me as I make my way toward Em and Diego's house.

"Why go outside if going through the clubhouse is faster?" I ask, genuinely curious.

"Stormy is single," he says, his eyes locked on the path in front of us.

"So am I," I say, loving the way his back stiffens.

"We also have three new members coming in soon."

"Em told me about them."

"If they flirt with you, don't take it personally."

"Because they couldn't possibly actually think I'm attractive?" I do my best to keep the irritation out of my tone, but I fail miserably.

The implication that they would flirt with me just to do it seems hateful to me.

"They aren't the type of guys you need to get involved with."

"And here I was thinking all the Cerberus members were elite men and women with the utmost integrity."

He frowns, his eyes darting between mine as I step onto the porch and turn to face him.

"We aren't exactly known for... You know what, never mind." He turns around and begins to walk away.

"I doubt anyone will flirt with me," I say to his back. "They'll probably just stare at my legs like you do."

I have no idea how he responds or if he does at all because I walk inside the house and quickly close the door.

Em isn't in the kitchen or living room, and Diego, I've found, stays pretty scarce when his wife isn't around. I head up to the room they've generously allowed me to stay in and begin pulling the clothes out of the bags. It takes me ten minutes to pull the tags from everything before I can carry them back down to the laundry room.

I nap while they wash, setting an alarm to switch it over to the dryer, and then continue the nap while they dry. I'm still exhausted from not sleeping at all while on the bus from Nebraska.

Em asks me if I want something to eat, but I decline, too excited to get started on upcycling the clothes to even pause on my way back upstairs.

I pull the large, pin-striped button-down out of the pile, putting it to the side and using the available hangers in the closet to hang everything else up.

I take my time on this first project, sewing, cutting, embellishing, grateful I found those super cute oversized sunflower buttons. Emmett may not have seen it that way, but the thrift store we went to was a treasure trove of great finds.

When the little dress is done, I carry it downstairs, finding Em in the kitchen washing a few dishes.

"Did you decide on dinner?" she asks, turning in my direction. "How cute is that?"

I beam with pride as I hold the dress up a little higher.

"It's for Millie."

"Did you find that while out shopping?"

"I made this from a man's shirt."

Her eyes dart from mine back to the dress, as if she can't believe what she's seeing. "Really?"

"Pretty cool, huh?"

"Incredible," she says. "I bet my girls would've loved something like this when they were little. Those buttons are just adorable."

"All of it only cost like three dollars."

That's the great thing about upcycling. You can source all of your supplies incredibly inexpensively.

"It's stunning." She allows the fabric to shift between her fingertips. "It looks like it was made for a retail store."

I take a deep breath, knowing if I don't take my chance to discuss my plans now, I may never have another one.

"I'd like to find a bank that's willing to give me a loan," I say. "Fashion is my dream, and I'd like to start my own business."

Em looks at me the way I imagine a mother who cared would look. "Honey, you aren't going to find a bank willing to invest, no matter how great your products are."

I deflate, my good mood instantly gone.

"But," she says, holding up her finger. "I know a few private investors who might be willing."

"Really?" I do my best not to sound too hopeful, but what I thought was going to be sheer disappointment has once again shifted.

"You'll need a business plan. How about you do some research and get it all together, and I'll see when they might be available for a meeting?"

I could literally cry right now, making me glad I didn't broach this topic of conversation while at the luncheon because I wouldn't have the privacy I need right now to shed a few tears of relief.

"I can do that," I assure her, a wide grin on my face.

Her chuckle tickles my back as I spin around to go back upstairs and get to work.

"Oh crap," I say, flying back down the stairs and holding the dress out to her. "Can you make sure Millie gets this?"

"Of course I can," she says, taking it from me.

I get very little sleep that night. I research business plans, fashion businesses, and educate myself a ton, familiarizing myself with the things that would make investors take a chance with me.

The thrill of getting all of this together keeps me motivated, but as the sun comes back up, the exhaustion creeps in. The house is still silent. Em and Diego are either still in bed or incredibly quiet, so I opt to take a nap before seeing if Em has a way of printing off everything I've done on my phone. Handwritten notes just won't do.

14

LEGACY

I haven't seen Devyn in three days, not since I took her shopping on Sunday. I've felt like a complete asshole, but warning her about how the new guys coming in may act wasn't received the way I meant it to be. I just don't want her thinking that any of the guys would want more from her than what she has between her legs. I know that's beyond harsh, but it's the truth. They aren't bad guys, but they aren't going to sleep with her and fall in love with her. She's young and probably doesn't understand that kind of stuff.

But what the hell do I know about girls or women? Honestly, not a damn thing.

What I do know is that I need to apologize. I probably should've done it before walking away on Sunday, but she floored me with her snapback about watching her legs. The woman is fiery and full of attitude, and I like it much more than I should. I don't know if she's avoiding me because of what I said or if I creeped her out with the way she caught me looking at her. I've considered going to her and promising I won't do it again, but I'm well aware of my limitations. There's just something about her that makes it impossible for me to maintain control of myself at times.

I shake my head, trying to do my best to rid it of the thoughts that have badgered me since that day. Remembering her smooth silky skin while she was sitting in the SUV won't impress whoever it is that opens the door. I lift my hand, knocking lightly on Kincaid's front door, my nerves deciding now to remind me that I still haven't figured out what I'm going to say to her.

I freeze, wholly unprepared when Kincaid pulls the door open.

"You don't have to knock," he says, holding his hand out.

I look down at the notebook-like spiral.

"Come on," he says, waving it until I pull it from his hand. "We're about to get started."

I feel out of place and unsure of what's happening, but curiosity wins out as I follow my boss into his living room.

Several other people are sitting around, all facing a small podium in the front.

I take a seat beside Max and look down at the front cover of the item Kincaid handed me before flipping through the pages. It isn't very long, but it's clear it's some sort of business proposal, the title *Devyn Malloy Designs* on the front. The logo is hand drawn and a little crude, but it's distinctly feminine and cute.

I grin as she enters the room, her cheeks pink with nerves. I quickly recognize the clothes she's wearing but only because it was originally one of the men's dress shirts I commented on being too large for her. Other than the red-checked pattern, nothing is the same. When she mentioned things needing to be altered, I had no idea she was planning to make a whole new outfit.

The dress is a little shorter than the one she had on the day she arrived, but it somehow still looks professional. She looks like the businesswoman I'm sure she intended to look like.

"Hello everyone," she says, her voice a squeak that requires her to clear her throat.

She apologizes under her breath.

Em is beaming like a proud mother, so it makes me believe she helped Devyn with this project.

Devyn begins by talking about her love for fashion and the things she's done to date in the field. Almost a little too late, I realize this is a loan proposal... one I didn't get invited to attend. Kincaid mistakenly took my arrival as participation when I just happened up at the right time.

Is she so mad at me that she didn't think I'd want to be involved?

I would've offered her money to pay for whatever endeavor she wanted to do, but she didn't ask me for money. She asked about a bank loan. It feels like every step I take where she's concerned is one more fuckup on my part.

I can't help how broody I feel as she continues her presentation. Her nerves are apparent, her hands shaking right along with the tremble in her voice. She's very knowledgeable, making it clear she's well-versed in the needs of her business.

I look around the room, seeing Kid's wife, Khloe, along with Harley and Alyssa. I've never even seen her speak to any of these people, so I know Em or Misty had to have been involved in arranging this opportunity for her. I can't help but feel a little jealous and a lot territorial over her. I want to provide all the help, but I keep my mouth closed.

It's clear she wants to create a successful, sustaining business and not just get handouts. I wouldn't be doing her any favors if I just threw money at her.

There's a hint of eagerness in her tone when she speaks about several paid project opportunities she's discovered online—one being a rather large order for some type of footballs. I'm not fully understanding exactly what you can do as far as footballs and fashion are concerned. Her passion for it makes me think she's capable of handling it.

Some of the spark leaves her eyes when she goes into speaking about overhead and the expense of completing the project as if she's already doubting every person in the room will help her.

"The initial investment just for this project would be over fifteen hundred dollars, not counting the cost of the footballs. If I can get a good deal on the sale of my sewing machine, then I can—"

"Wouldn't you need the sewing machine for the other projects you spoke of?" Khloe asks.

Devyn gives her a soft yet clearly forced smile, her chin quivering as she answers. "Yes, ma'am."

She looks a little defeated, and I want to dive in and save the day, but I know I won't have to. She may not know these people, but I do, and they won't let her fail.

"Who wants the football order?" Kincaid asks.

Devyn refers to a small notebook, before answering. "Phil Benson."

Kincaid nods before pulling his phone out of his pocket, making me wonder if he knows the guy.

"You mentioned upcycling and alterations," Max begins. "Does that include men's clothing?"

"Yes," she answers quickly.

"You'll be able to use the embroidery machine for more than just sports equipment, right?" Alyssa asks.

"Of course. It can be used on clothing, towels, hats. The options are endless."

"I imagine you'll need a website and e-Commerce site," Max says. "I'd like to trade that for alterations. Tug's slacks are too loose around the waist because he has to buy a larger size to accommodate his thigh muscles."

"I do need a website," she says with a timid smile.

"I'd like to purchase the embroidery machine you'll need, but not the one you suggested. With helping you with this presentation, I did a little research. I found that it's suggested to get the commercial machine rather than the novice, at-home model you were planning to get," Em says.

"That's very expensive," she whispers.

"In exchange, I'd like you to make some more one-of-a-kind clothes for the kiddos at the shelter. Millie's dress made several others jealous, and I'd like to see smiles on all their faces."

"I'd love to do that, but you don't have to spend all that money—"

Em holds up her hand. "That's how I'd like to invest in your brand."

"We're having a Polar Express evening with the daycare kids," Alyssa says. "I was thinking of matching parent and kid jammies. Isn't that a great idea, babe?"

Harley nods, a forced smile on his face as if it's far from a great idea, but I know the man will wear anything Alyssa suggests. The guy is a goner for that woman.

Devyn is writing all of this down in her notebook.

"I think we could handle the initial investment of footballs for that one order in exchange," Alyssa continues.

"My anniversary is coming up, and I'd like my wedding dress altered into a party dress for the party," Khloe says.

"You still fit into your wedding dress?" Em asks, looking a little sad and a whole lot jealous.

"What did I tell you about that shit?" Kincaid growls, his voice low as he leans in close to his wife. "You're fucking perfect."

"Only because it was a little big on me, remember?" Khloe offers.

"I can do wedding dress alterations," Devyn says, drawing the attention back to her.

"I can do a monetary investment to be used at your discretion in exchange," Khloe offers.

Devyn swallows with a nod, jotting down that information in her notebook.

She looks like she's on the verge of tears, ecstatic that people are speaking up and investing in her dreams.

"I'd like to do a cash advance as well," I speak up.

Instead of looking up and meeting my eyes, she keeps her head lowered long after the pen stops moving over the paper.

"In exchange for what?" Kincaid asks when it becomes clear that Devyn doesn't plan on speaking up.

"Umm," I say, scratching nervously at the back of my neck.

A few things come to mind, and I fight those thoughts off because this isn't the place for it. I doubt there will ever be a right time.

"I don't think I have any sewing needs." I ignore Max's chuckles. "But I can go through my closet in the next couple of days."

I know I have a few shirts missing buttons, but I don't speak up about them.

"She'll need to be transported on occasion," Kincaid says.

"There are some fabulous fabric stores in Albuquerque," Khloe adds.

"Even better ones in Denver," Em replies.

I nod, trying not to think about how Denver is so far away it requires an overnight stay.

"I'll give her a ride wherever she wants to go."

"I bet," Max mutters. I'm grateful he's sitting right beside me, and it seems no one else heard him.

I fight the urge to jab him in the side because it would be childish, but no more childish than him spouting off at the mouth.

15

Devyn

"Still no word?"

I shake my head.

After the meeting, Em assured me people were going to invest in Devyn Malloy Designs even if I didn't get the order for the embroidered footballs. She ordered the machine last night, stating that I'll need it for Alyssa and Harley's investment, anyway.

I spent a few hours yesterday after the meeting making a few more dresses for some of the girls at the shelter and then went over online fabric choices for the pajamas Alyssa wanted me to make. I was glad she didn't find pre-made pajamas that she liked because it gives me the opportunity to make each of them. It speaks to my fashion heart to do so. It'll take a week before that fabric is delivered. I've always hated the waiting game part of everything.

I open my mouth, but my phone chimes with a notification. I do my best to remain calm when I see Mr. Benson's name at the top of the text thread.

Mr. Benson: The Farmington Peewee Football organization would like to formally accept your proposition on our project, but there's an issue with the price.

My heart races. I knew better than to ask what I did, but Em assured me my original price was too low.

My phone chimes again.

Mr. Benson: With the price of footballs, we'll need you to adjust the individual price from your offer of $30 per ball to $50 per ball.

I blink down at the text. What person in their right mind would demand to pay more?

"What's that look for?"

"He wants to pay me twenty dollars extra per ball than I bid."

Em smiles. "Fifty is still a great price for them. They're selling for sixty and higher online."

"I can't believe it."

"Believe it," Em insists. "Phil is also the one in charge of both the softball and baseball leagues in town. Play your cards right and he may order some of those cute baseballs we saw online while doing research."

My heart flutters with excitement as I text back, letting him know I'm thrilled to get started.

We text back and forth, ironing out all the details, and I feel like a real business owner when he says he'll email over the contract.

"He's going to email the contract, and after it's signed, he's going to make a fifty percent down payment."

"You should have Faith look over the contract. She's a lawyer."

I frown. "Will he try to cheat me somehow?"

"Not a chance," she assures me. "But it's a good practice to get into. Plus, Faith mentioned a wonky hemline on one of her dresses a few days ago, and it never hurts to have an attorney on retainer. She'll be here tomorrow for the get-together we're having for the new guys, which reminds me. The rooms will need to be refreshed."

I follow her out of the house, feeling light on my feet. My world is looking up. For the first time in a long time, I'm ecstatic about my future. I may have had doubts about coming to New Mexico, but it's proving to be the best decision of my life.

"The cleaning supplies are in here," Em says, opening a door in the hallway. "It's going to be those three rooms on that end."

I nod, my eyes following the point of her fingers.

"Laundry pods are in the cabinet above the washer. Any questions?"

I shake my head, wanting to give her a hug and thank her for all of her help.

For the first time in my life, I have a smile on my face while facing household chores. She said everyone earns their keep, but honestly, she's done more for me than I even knew to ask for. I'd gladly scrub these floors with a two-bristle toothbrush if that's what she wanted. Fortunately, she has a mop and bucket instead.

I carry supplies to the furthest room and then proceed to strip the bed, moving to the next room to do the same. It's going to take more than one trip to the laundry room, so I know it's also going to take multiple loads. I realize it won't be as many as I suspected because the washers—yes plural—and dryers are commercial sized, much larger than residential machines.

"Nice," I say, the sheets and pillowcases from all three beds fitting inside one machine, leaving the other two washers available for the comforters.

With the wash going, I head back to the first room. With my hands on my hips, I decide that the bathroom would be the best place to start. I pop in my earbuds, selecting an upbeat playlist from the music app on my phone, and get to work.

I'm jamming along to one of my favorite songs in the second room, using the mop handle as a microphone, when my impromptu dance takes me into a spin.

I scream louder than necessary, I'm sure, at the sight of Emmett in the doorway, leaning against the frame with a wide grin on his face.

I rip one of the earbuds from my ear to stop the music, my chest heaving from my energetic cleaning.

"Do you need some help in here?"

I shake my head. "I'm earning my keep."

His eyes lock on my mouth as I speak. Some of the boys in high school would do that. The ones with manners would eventually look away. The disgusting ones would make suggestions on what a girl's mouth was good for.

I swallow, wondering if I'd be offended if he made the same suggestions.

"Is that something guys never grow out of?"

"What's that?" he asks, his tongue tucking into the corner of his mouth, his eyes still locked on mine.

"Watching a woman's mouth while she speaks?"

His eyes dart up to mine, making me believe he was doing it more out of instinct than conscious thought.

"The boys at school at least had the balls to say something about it rather than staring like a creep."

"Teenage boys are young, dumb, and full of cum, Devyn. They only have one thing on their minds."

"And it's not the same thing you have on yours right now?" I challenge, my great mood giving me more bravery than I'd normally have, as I drop my eyes to the front of his jeans. It leaves me wondering if he got aroused watching me dance around like an idiot or if that's just his unaroused bulge. Either way, it seems impressive.

I want to squeal in feminine victory when he shifts his weight from one foot to the other.

He clears his throat, pulling my eyes back up to his.

"Maybe I'm wrong about your attraction to me."

"You're not wrong," he says, shocking the hell out of me. "It's wrong. The attraction that is," he adds, stepping further into the room. "Vaughn wouldn't approve. I'm too old for you."

"I think that's a matter of opinion," I say, a hint of something I don't fully understand in my voice.

"I was there the day your parents brought you home from the hospital. It's weird."

"Wow," I mutter, turning to dip the mop back into the bucket of cleaning solution. "Shit, I get it. Don't have to call me weird."

"I said my attraction to you is weird. It makes me feel weird," he clarifies.

"And you making a big deal about our age difference makes it sound like you disapprove. You weren't there while I was growing up. I don't have daddy issues." That may not be completely true. I have a lot of issues with my parents, the biggest being that they acted as if losing one child meant they forfeited me too. "I think if we're attracted to each other, we should date and see where it goes. But if your hangups are that big then that's fine, too. Just stop watching me like you want a taste. It messes with my head."

"Want a taste," he mutters, and I can tell by the way he says it, it's for his benefit, not mine. "It's inappropriate and can never happen."

"I'm not a virgin," I say, turning around to face him. He once again has to snap his eyes up from my legs to my face. "But maybe you already guessed that. Is that why you aren't interested? Are you into innocent virgins, Emmett?"

I know getting an attitude and taunting him probably isn't the best way to get what I want, but I can't seem to stop the words from tumbling out of my mouth.

Instead of sticking around to argue, he shakes his head and walks away.

I pop my ear bud back in. This time when the music takes over, I add a little extra sway to my hips just in case he stops back by.

16

LEGACY

I thought walking away after what she said was the best plan. I had no intention of spending the night tossing and turning because each step that carried me away from her felt like the wrong decision.

I'm in a horrible mood as I climb out of the shower. The soft towel feels like a scouring pad on my skin, and ignoring my cock while I was bathing has now become an apparent wrong choice. Something I seem to be a fan of these days.

I shove my legs into jeans, still pissed, but I'm a grown-ass man. I've got bigger issues to worry about if I allow myself to be controlled by an erection. I couldn't jack off without her flashing into my mind, and she was right. I either need to take a step forward or leave her the fuck alone. This limbo sucks for both of us, and admitting I was attracted to her doesn't solve a damn thing. Gripping my cock in my hand in the shower is the equivalent of someone declining dessert at dinner with friends, claiming they're on a diet, only to binge eat an entire cheesecake when they get home. Doing it under the cover of darkness with no witnesses doesn't make it okay either.

Cheesecake makes me think of strawberry drizzle, and fuck if my horny mind doesn't force me to picture the tips of Devyn's tits coated in sweet, sticky sauce, begging to be licked off.

I clench my fists several times before reaching out to open the bedroom door. I know if I stay in my room, I'll pull my cock out, and probably gasp her fucking name as I come. I can't fucking have that, now can I?

The voice in my head that always pushes me toward temptation tells me it's fine. That voice has been the loudest of all since the moment Devyn arrived at the clubhouse. Thinking of Vaughn's sister like that makes me feel like I'm betraying my friend's memory.

The kitchen is busy, people bustling around, working on preparations for the party this evening, where we'll be welcoming the newest members of Cerberus. I sort of feel like I know Hemlock, Oracle, and Newton already from the bios we went over as a group last week. Reading their information felt a little invasive, but I know everyone before me did the same with mine. Maybe it's because I'm from the most recent group of guys to join, and it's still really new for me. The new guys will no doubt be nervous. I know I was, despite what happened that first night.

The night Bishop, Stormy, and I arrived, Ugly was drugged, and it set into motion a whole fucking array of shit that included a serial killer and the murder of several women. Not to mention Bishop being drugged and left in a coma for over a month. I think everyone is hoping for a less eventful welcome this time around.

My eyes immediately find Devyn even though I have no damn business looking in her direction.

It makes me a misogynistic asshole for getting annoyed that she's not a virgin. I don't blame anyone for it. She's an adult after all, but I still hate whatever man got that piece of her. I don't even know anything about him, but I know he didn't deserve it. No one, including myself, would be worthy of that gift.

The dress she's wearing, another upcycled invention no doubt, teases the back of her thighs. Although I'm not a man too big on fashion, I've paid enough attention to her to know that I haven't seen the little bootie shoe things she's wearing before. I'll be mad if I find out someone else took her shopping. I agreed to be the one to take her places in exchange for my investment. If I've been robbed of an opportunity, I'll be livid.

Once again I cross the room, choosing to take a seat on the side of the table that will leave me facing those in the kitchen. Stormy has that same knowing grin on his face that he always has when I'm in the same room as Devyn. Discreetly, I flip him the bird, this type of interaction becoming common these days.

"Still hard up for that one, huh?" Stormy asks before I can sit down.

I glare at him, wondering how far his voice traveled.

Kincaid would skin us both if we made anyone in here feel uncomfortable.

"Would you leave it alone?"

He shakes his head, grinning like the asshole he is. "Are you really going to keep fighting it this hard?"

"There's nothing to fight."

"The way the two of you watch each other says differently."

"She watches me?"

He chuckles, and I know I just failed some type of test.

"Asshole," I grumble under my breath when he chuckles. "But seriously, does she watch me?"

"Do you know how many issues can be solved by people just talking to one another? We'd probably have a cure for cancer and a solution for world hunger and world peace."

Instead of staying in the kitchen being forced to listen to him, I stand back up. Like the pest that he is, Stormy stands as well.

I don't know if it's my imagination or what, but I feel like her eyes are on me when I leave the kitchen.

"You really think everyone will leave her alone if you don't claim her?" Stormy asks as we head out the front door of the clubhouse and take a right off the porch toward the garage.

"She isn't a piece of furniture," I mutter. "Claiming people isn't a thing."

"Yet you were incredibly quick to step in front of me when I volunteered to marry her if you don't."

"I'm not marrying her," I assure him, growling when he opens his mouth to speak. "And you sure as fuck aren't either."

"I would," he says, his tone growing suddenly serious. "If that's what she needed. I'd do that."

"You don't even fucking know her," I argue, my feet feeling like a million pounds.

"Don't have to know her to see how beautiful she is, and she's young. I bet she's eager to please."

I spin on him, my fists automatically tangling in the fabric of his t-shirt.

"If you don't get her out of your thoughts, I'm going to beat your ass until you can't even remember your own name."

"Is there a problem here?"

I release Stormy the second I hear Kid's voice.

"Just proving a point," Stormy says, his grin still in place as he straightens his shirt.

"And that would be?" Kid asks.

"Legacy has claimed Devyn."

"I thought that was a given?" Kid says looking at me. "Aren't you two getting married?"

Stormy chuckles, making me wonder what the consequences of punching him in front of one of my bosses would be.

Instead of taking the chance, I walk away, both of them laughing as I enter the garage like they know more than I do about my own damn life.

It's early afternoon, but since I have nowhere to be but here, I grab a beer from the fridge and drop my ass into one of the chairs. Stormy follows suit. I'd apologize for putting my hands on him, but he still has that smug-as-hell look on his face.

We sit in silence for fifteen minutes until we hear the crunch of gravel.

Stormy pops up first, but I'm not far behind him.

Kincaid climbs out of the passenger seat of the SUV as Shadow, our VP, climbs out from behind the wheel. The rear doors open, three guys piling out and looking around in amazement.

It's easy to think back to doing this very same thing months ago when I first arrived.

We're introduced to them and vice versa as several more of the guys pile out of the clubhouse.

"Wow," Newton says.

"You'll get used to all the people," I assure him.

"I'm going to feel like a jerk not remembering everyone's names."

"We won't hold it against you," Stormy says. "It's quite overwhelming and there's twice as many people inside."

In the time that we were sitting in the garage, others have walked across from their houses on the opposite side of the road from the clubhouse. The living room is packed with people.

"Just mingle and have a good time," Kincaid assures them as we walk inside. "This isn't a test. We want you comfortable here."

Hemlock looks around, his lips a flat line. If I didn't know the extensive vetting the Cerberus guys do for him to get to this point, I'd think he was a criminal. His dark beard and assessing eyes make him damn near unapproachable. Maybe he's just as overwhelmed as any of us were, and seeming unapproachable is just how he deals with those kinds of stress.

"Legacy," I tell him, holding my hand out.

He looks down at it, the action making me think he's going to refuse to shake my hand.

"Hemlock," he says after giving my hand one pump and releasing it. "Is it always so busy?"

I turn and look around the room. "Not always, but we do have a lot of gatherings. Em, that's Kincaid's wife, likes a lot of socialization among everyone, so she's always got a party of some kind planned."

"Are they a requirement for the job?"

His question floors me. We all come from a Marine background. The military isn't a solo operation. We're always in teams. Cerberus is no different.

"I don't think so, but—"

"Kincaid said my room is the one at the end of the hall. You got any idea where that is?" he interrupts.

I tilt my head to the side. I've met a lot of brusque people in my lifetime. Some guys don't give a shit what people think of them. They are who they are and make no excuses for it. It seems Hemlock is going to fall into that category.

"I can show you," I tell him, only now realizing he's the only one of the new trio that carried his duffel inside.

He falls into line behind me, following me from the room. I point to his closed door.

"That one. It's been recently cleaned."

He nods in my direction, a token of appreciation rather than wasting his breath, and then heads in that direction.

His door opens and closes with a light click, making me wonder if he has any plans to rejoin the party.

I make my way back out to the living room, honestly a little glad he'll be on Team A with Stormy rather than my team.

"Did he say more to you?" Newton asks as he approaches me.

"Not much."

"He literally didn't say a word on the drive here."

"All of this can be a little much," I say, still giving the guy the benefit of the doubt.

He tilts his head as if he agrees, but it still may not apply to that new guy.

"You like it here?" Newton asks, his eyes canvassing the room as he lifts a bottle of water to his lips.

"It's an amazing organization. The guys are—" My words freeze when I see Oracle walking toward Devyn. "You know anything about him?"

"Other than he's the cockiest guy I've ever met? No. That your girl?"

As much as I'd like to claim her like Stormy suggested, I'd look like a complete idiot if I did that and she ends up flirting with the guy right in front of us.

"She's from my past," I confess. "Showed up here a week or so ago. She needed a little help."

"Gonna threaten him, too?" Stormy asks, having seen Oracle's approach to her as well.

"I'm starting to think you're stalking me," I mutter, wishing I'd grabbed a beer so I have something to do with my hands rather than just clenching them repeatedly at my sides.

"A stalker stalking a stalker," he says with a grin. "What a concept."

"So she is your girl?" Newton asks.

It's my turn to glare at the guy. I swear I knew this was going to happen. I warned Devyn about this. I shouldn't be surprised that two of the three new guys have already set their sights on her. Every other man in the room who has a significant other is keeping them very close, claiming them with their actions, either an arm around their waist or holding their hands. Devyn is the only one wandering around without someone beside her, and these guys are astute as the next.

"You guys planning on going to *Jake's*?" I ask, a hint that the women here aren't the only ones that exist in the world.

"Didn't work out so well last time," Stormy mutters, referring to the first time we showed up here and went out that same night.

"I don't drink," Newton says.

"They sell Cokes, too," Stormy says, making it sound like he's going tonight regardless of what happened last time.

I turn my eyes, catching another glimpse of Devyn, only to find her and Oracle looking in my direction. He raises an eyebrow at me, and it feels like he's seeking some form of confirmation.

When I stand still, with no reaction, his grin grows, a glint in his eyes that says if I don't claim her that makes her fair game.

It pisses me off when it really shouldn't.

I know Dr. Alverez, the club's psychologist, would tell me that my feelings are just... mine, and I have every right to feel what I feel.

Instead of doing something to make me jealous or push me into action like I assumed someone as young as Devyn would do, she simply looks disappointed, taking a step back when Oracle inches forward.

It's just another way that she's proving me wrong. Her maturity is showing, and that doesn't help my insistence on staying away from her.

17

Devyn

"I'd love to do that for you," I tell Sunshine.

"I know you're busy, but everyone has been so excited about all their custom things." She presses her hand to her nearly flat stomach. "We have time, but I figured custom curtains and throw pillows in the nursery would be amazing."

My smile grows wider, but then I see the unspoken things in her eyes. If I had to wager, I imagine she's just now at a point in her life where she can do things like order custom curtains and pillows. I met her fiancé, Bishop, one of the guys in Cerberus, a little earlier, and I could easily tell the man would give her the world before she even needed to ask for it.

I fight the urgency to find that type of life for myself. I'm not exactly interested in being a mom. I'm sure I'd be horrible at it because I didn't have the best example, but I want the type of love so many people here have found. I want to see the dedicated and utter devotion in a man's eyes when he looks in my direction.

"I'll make sure to add it to my list, but I assure you, I'll have it done before your sweet little baby is born."

She squeezes my hand as if I'm the one doing her a favor when in actuality, her placing an order with me is the true gift.

So many people have come up to me to ask about things I can do for them, and I've taken every single order. I'll work through the night if I have to. No one has asked for a discount. Many are like Sunshine and didn't even ask what the price would be, but I haven't once gotten the vibe that any of them are expecting it for free.

Everyone who invested in Devyn Malloy Designs has done it on a one-off arrangement, meaning I don't owe anyone a percentage of my business after their items have been made. Em didn't specify a set number of one-of-a-kind clothes for the children at the shelter, but I know she won't abuse it by expecting me to make clothes forever. I would though because her buying the embroidery machine in order for me to win the football bid was epic.

I look around the room, excitement flowing through my veins. I can't wait to get started on all the projects. My fingers are itching to run through some fabric.

I avoid the side of the room where Emmett is speaking with someone. It's possible he's one of the new guys, but I haven't met everyone yet, so I'm not a hundred percent sure.

"Hi."

I turn my head, a smile already on my lips.

"Hello," I say, a little nervous from the obviously flirtatious smile on his lips.

He holds his hand out, and courtesy has me shaking it.

"I'm Oracle."

"Devyn," I return politely.

He takes longer than needed to release my hand. Although I don't get a weird, creepy vibe from him, I'm also not interested in him flirting with me either.

Emmett is attracted to me. He said as much yesterday. I know he's going to try to avoid me, as if the man is stubborn enough to think that not being around me will make it go away. Doesn't he know that absence makes the heart grow fonder or however the saying goes?

Then again, as much as I want to think I know him, I could be way off. I can assume he's an honorable man, but him not wanting to jump on the opportunity to feed his attraction to me doesn't necessarily make him honorable either.

"I predict things," Oracle says when I do nothing to further the conversation.

I'm not trying to be rude by not making small talk with him, but he's not exactly the person in the room I wish was standing in front of me right now.

"Want me to predict things about you?"

I look in Emmett's direction, wanting him to come over and join this conversation, but he seems locked in place.

Oracle follows my gaze. "He your guy?"

"Would saying yes make you stop flirting?"

He presses his hand to his chest. "You wound me, Devyn."

My lips tug up in a half-smile, the silly tone of his voice speaking deeply to that part of me that feeds on attention from others.

Oracle and Emmett share some sort of man look. Although I don't fully understand it, I get the feeling Emmett just somehow gave Oracle permission to proceed, that flirting with me would be okay.

Oracle is full on smiling at me now, despite the glare I send in Emmett's direction. He doesn't look exactly happy, but he isn't coming over here to put a stop to it either.

I feel traded, discarded. Any thought I had about him fighting his attraction to me slips away. Maybe he figures it would be easier to get past it if someone else is in the way, but I'll be damned if I'm going to let him off the hook that easily.

"That guy's old," Oracle says.

"He's only thirty," I mutter.

"That's ancient. I'm only twenty-six. How old are you?"

I lift my chin a little higher. "Eighteen."

He slow blinks at me, as if struggling with the information.

"Are you the daughter of one of the Cerberus guys?"

He looks around nervously as if he fully expects one of the guys to jump out and grab him up by the shirt collar and demand to know what his intentions are with me.

"I'm not."

His face transforms once again. As distracting as it is, I still can't seem to give him all my attention.

It's clear Emmett isn't going to make a move, and I've never been one to waste my time.

"What were you saying about predictions?"

He tries his best to maintain his smile, but I can see some of the enthusiasm drain out.

"It wouldn't work now," he says, shifting on his feet.

"What's that?"

"The punchline. I say *want me to predict things about you?* And you say *sure*, and then I say something like *I predict your clothes on my bedroom floor* and you say—"

"Hold on." I reach my hand out and place it on his forearm to silence him. "That kind of shit works on women?"

His grin grows wider. "Usually. You're sure you're eighteen?"

A chuckle bubbles out of my mouth. "That's a horrible pickup line. Did you give yourself that nickname? Please tell me you did. That would make this so much funnier."

He releases a good-natured laugh. "I didn't, but now I'm kind of wishing I did. I think I like you, Devyn. You're a breath of fresh air."

"You know those lines aren't going to work on me, right?"

"I know you're too beautiful not to try."

"Thank you," I tell him, pushing a lock of hair behind my ear, watching his eyes follow the movement. I swear guys are so easy.

Maybe Emmett was right about boys because it doesn't seem like Oracle has fully grown up yet.

"He's a lucky man," he says.

"Who?" I ask.

"I'm not sure what the game is, but it's working."

"What are you—"

"We didn't finalize our plans yesterday," Emmett says as he steps up and inserts himself into our conversation.

Oracle grins, taking a step back.

"And what plans would those be?" There's more than a hint of irritation in my voice.

Emmett shouldn't be approaching me because he's jealous of another man, and using our conversation from yesterday is a low blow seeing as he was so quick to walk away from it. It's childish, and that's something coming from the guy who claims I'm too young for him.

I fight the urge to cross my arms over my chest and kick out an irritated foot because I'm trying to be the mature one.

"We'll talk later about a few more predictions I have," Oracle says, winking in my direction before walking away.

"That guy is no good for you," Emmett says, his eyes on me instead of watching the new Cerberus member walk away to join another group of people.

"You mentioned going on a date and seeing where it goes." His nervousness is apparent when he clutches at the back of his neck, pulling his hand down as if he's trying to work out some tension that has built up there.

I tilt my head, scrunching up my nose.

"Do you really think I'm going to fall for this?"

"Fall for what?" He looks equally confused.

"You see another guy talking to me, and out of jealousy, you come over here and try to make your move?" I shake my head. "No, Emmett. If you weren't capable of stepping up before there was competition, why would I jump at the opportunity you're providing now? Grow up."

I walk away, knowing it's a gamble, knowing there's a very real chance the man may never ask me out again, but I can't tell him yes even though my heart is racing in my chest.

I put myself out there with him, and he shot me down. I'm not going to get all giddy and jump for joy because he felt the need to approach me when he saw another man talking to me.

I spend the rest of the gathering skirting the larger groups. Emmett doesn't come up to me again, but his distance doesn't keep others from approaching either. By the time the party dwindles, many of the folks with kids leaving not long after the sun faded out of the sky, I have a list of new orders. I had to start telling people I'd have to schedule their projects, but not one person gave me the impression they expected to be pushed to the front of the line.

Although I've kept my distance, I'm always aware of where he is in the room. I can't control that part of me that keeps looking in his direction. It's how I see the defeat in him take over.

My heart clenches painfully when I see him drop his eyes and turn toward the hallway leading to his room.

18

LEGACY

I'm thirty years old, meaning by my age, I've made more mistakes than I can count, but this dread inside of me that I may have made the biggest one yet is louder than the din of the party.

She shot me down and then spent the rest of the evening chatting with people. I swear, even from across the room, I could hear the tinkle of her laughter. It's clear she isn't in the middle of a performance. She isn't doing anything that makes me feel like she's purposely trying to torture me, but that still doesn't change the fact that she is.

I tell Newton goodnight, ignoring Stormy's chuckle as I walk away and head for my room. Maybe I'll be given a chance to apologize to her tomorrow, but I doubt she'll ever agree to date me. I consider my thoughts on her being too young, but it seems like I'm the immature one here.

"Emmett."

I spin in the direction of her voice, fully considering the possibility that I'm hallucinating right now.

Her cheeks are flushed as she approaches me. I know she hasn't been drinking, and the distance between here and where she was standing when I left the room isn't too great.

I want to raise my hand, brush my thumb over the heat on her face, and ask her why she's so flushed.

I chalk it up to nerves. There's just something about that thought that makes my dick threaten to pay more attention. What is it about a woman's inexperience that makes a man want to go all alpha and take charge?

"I umm," she says, stepping a little closer to me.

I swear I'd be able to taste the sugar on her lips from the soda she was drinking earlier if she got any closer.

My throat works on a swallow, my own set of nerves taking the opportunity to flare up.

Jesus, it would be so easy to just loop my arm around her back and pull her against me. The urge to do so reminds me of how perfectly her body fit against mine when I stopped her from falling when I took her shopping. I can't recall a single other moment in all my life when I wanted someone so badly.

Is it because it's a little taboo? Because she's forbidden? Is it because doing something so bad would feel so good?

I shake my head, realizing it has nothing to do with any of that. My attraction to her has nothing to do with the devious side of me, that little devil voice in my head shoving me toward temptation.

It's her, a hundred percent. There's just something about Devyn Malloy that speaks to me on a molecular level. It tells me that avoiding her will be impossible, no matter how hard I try.

"Devyn," I whisper, urging her to speak.

"Don't," she says, pressing her palm to my chest.

The muscles jump under her hand, drawing her eyes there. I swear the slow look down and the even slower look back up send tendrils of fire through every inch of my body.

I lick my lips, wanting to taste every damn inch of her body.

"Let me get this out before I lose the nerve." She clears her throat, a nervous gesture that makes me want to do the same. "I want to take you up on your offer. I think a date would be nice."

"It was your offer," I argue. "Well, it was your idea first."

"Are we really going to argue semantics right now?" Her fingers flex over my shirt, the warmth of her hand somehow settling deeper inside of me.

I shake my head, thinking that this woman could tell me to do anything right now, and I'd probably do it with a smile.

"Are you not going to answer me?"

I blink down at her, my mind racing to try and remember the question she asked. It takes longer than it should, but I could easily blame her proximity for why my brain seems to have fried.

I almost tell her no. The reasons I turned her down yesterday still stand, but I know how big of a damn mistake that would be. She's offering me a do-over, and I'll be damned if I walk away again. I have no doubt she'd never be this vulnerable with me again.

But I have to consider what it means to say yes as well.

I know I'm physically attracted to her. The girl is smoking fucking hot, and every single guy in the room tonight knows it too. Is the connection purely physical? Am I just in need of getting laid? Is it because

I want to hold on to that connection I lost with Vaughn all those years ago? If she were a different person, having no connection to my past, would I still feel the same way?

I'd never hurt her just to get her in bed. I'm not that kind of guy, but what if it doesn't work out? What if I get to know her, and we aren't as compatible as my body is insisting that we are?

"I'd like that," I finally manage.

"You'd like to answer me?"

"I'd like to take you on a date."

Her shoulders relax some, the tension in them fading away.

"I won't have time to go out anytime soon," she says, looking nervous again as if I'd tell her now or never. "I have a lot of stuff being delivered tomorrow, and I have to get things setup. I took a million more orders tonight, and I don't know if I'll even have time to sleep for the next several weeks much less have time to go out and—"

I press my finger to her lips, hushing her.

I swear on everything holy if she keeps looking up at me the way she is, we'll end up in my bed on the other side of the door we're standing near.

"I'll be ready when you have time."

Fuck if I'm not ready for a hundred different things right now, but I can't take this where my body is insisting it goes. My prayer, deep down, is that we go out and discover we aren't at all compatible. Acting on attraction is one thing, and I'm strong enough to fight that part of it, but it would be entirely less messy if we discovered this wouldn't work out between us. Her parents hate me enough already.

"I want to go soon, but I also have all these other obligations," she continues against the press of my finger.

"It can wait," I assure her, part of me hoping the attraction fades between now and when her availability opens up.

"I'm trying to be mature about—"

"Devyn—"

"I don't want you to think—"

Even with the raging voice in my head telling me to take a step back, I pull my finger from her lips and replace it with my mouth.

The sound of her surprised gasp takes me from semi to full hard-on in a split second. Jesus, if I'm not the most wishy-washy fucking man on earth right now.

My reaction to her is borderline primal. I want to lift her up and pull her body against mine. I want to unzip my jeans and slip my cock between the lips of her pussy and push inside of her right here in the fucking hallway. I want to watch her eyes roll into the back of her head all the while her face contorts in the unavoidable pain of seating myself fully inside of her.

The tentative swipe of her tongue against mine has the power to make me lose my mind, and that's why I pull away rather than continuing.

I'm fucking breathless as I pull back and press my lips to her cheek.

"Sorry. I shouldn't have done that."

It isn't until her fingers flex that I realize she's clasped both hands in the fabric of my shirt. My arm is around her back, our bodies only a breath away.

"I'm not sorry," she says, the grip of her fingers tugging against my clothes when I take a step back.

"You should go," I tell her, more than half of me wishing she'd refuse.

This won't go the way it probably should if she can't be the stronger person right now. I know my limitations, and fighting this insistent urge to get her under me is only going to last so long.

"I don't want to," she whispers, but she takes a step back, her reluctant fingers taking even longer to release my shirt.

"I'll see you tomorrow?"

"Hopefully," she says before turning to walk back down the hallway.

The sound of the outside world doesn't come back into focus until after she's disappeared around the corner. The party is still going. People are chatting. There's soft music playing from the stereo system.

I heard none of it the entire time she was in front of me.

I'm in so much damned trouble.

19

Devyn

"I love the excitement," Em says as I follow her into the clubhouse.

I don't bother trying to resist rubbing my hands together. She told me several items were delivered earlier this morning.

We head down the hallway to the area known as the old rooms, despite them looking amazing. I should know. I cleaned three of them earlier this week.

"Did someone put them in one of the bedrooms?" I ask because I figured we'd head to the living room or the front porch. I was already trying to figure out how I was going to get the embroidery machine up the stairs in Em's house. If I move the dresser in there over a few feet, I will have room to set it up. I measured yesterday to make sure I had enough room.

"I had Emmett put them in here," she says, reaching for the doorknob to one of the rooms I didn't clean.

I step around her into the room, but it looks nothing like the three nearly identical rooms I helped freshen up a few days ago. There's no bed. In its place is a sturdy-looking worktable with several packages spread out on it.

"We figured you needed a little room to spread out. Plus, you need personal time. From what I already know about you, you'd never take that time if your work was surrounding you in your bedroom."

I scan the room, my mind already evaluating how I can set it up to get the most use out of the space.

"Emmett said he'd put the tables together," Em says, pointing to the corner of the room my eyes haven't made it to yet. "The other things are purchases from investors that you'll need to be successful."

I read the side of a thread rack box, realizing there is so much I didn't even realize I'd need.

"It's too much," I whisper.

"Your work is going to pay for all of this. It isn't a handout," Em explains. "Khloe's dress is hanging in the closet for that order. You have a box there that has fabric in it, and I suspect it's for the matching pajamas you're making for the Polar Express event."

I look toward the point of her finger, wanting to squeal in delight at the sight of the huge box. I've never been able to order entire bolts of fabric before.

"And the cutting table has an arm that pulls out when you need it and folds away when not in use so you have more space in the room."

"Em," I whisper, my eyes burning with tears. "I don't know how to say thank you."

"It's nothing," she says, waving her hand at me despite the wetness of her own eyes.

I shake my head. "It's everything to me."

I take a chance, stepping closer and wrapping my arms around her. A sob bubbles out of my throat when she wraps her arms all the way around me and holds me to her chest. It's everything I didn't know I needed. Her motherly attention feeds that part of me that has gone so long without it.

Em doesn't budge or grow fidgety. She simply holds on to me as long as I hold on to her. When I step back, she swipes at the tears on my cheeks before palming my face in both hands.

"I have no idea what you've been through, but you deserve success. There isn't one person who helped invest in this that doubts your abilities."

I nod, accepting her words because she's never given me any reason not to.

"Now get to work. You have a lot to do."

I nod, sniffling as she backs out of the room. The tears continue to fall to the point that I have to go into the en suite to grab some tissue paper to blow my nose and wash my face.

I take a deep fortifying breath as I step back into the room. As excited as I am, I'm also overwhelmed. My project list is long, and yet I can tell by looking around the room that it's very possible I don't have everything I need to fulfill a single order. I sure as hell can't do anything until this room is orderly.

I leave the boxes with the furniture in them alone, my breath growing a little uneven as I think about the interaction with Emmett last night in the hallway. I have a ton of things I could lose sleep over, but last night, my mind stayed hyper focused on that man. My head ran through scenarios of what could happen if he snuck up to my room in the middle of the night. My cheeks flare with heat at the memories of how those thoughts made me feel.

I take another deep breath, needing to get that out of my head if I have any hope of focusing on my tasks rather than fighting the urge to go corner him and demand he kiss me again.

I find a planner sitting on the corner of the desk, and more tears threaten to leak out when I see the handwritten note tucked inside the first page.

You were always meant to do great things. I rub my finger over Em's signature, wondering what I did in life to find such a welcoming, caring bunch of people.

I fight the urge to sit down and pull up the notes app on my phone to get the orders I've taken into the planner. I know I can work on that later this evening when my feet are screaming at me to take a break.

Like a kid on Christmas, I rush to open all the boxes so I can inventory what I have and what I might be missing. I want to kiss whoever thought of cube shelving that has versatile assembly options. They're positively genius. After getting them together and on one wall of the room, I'm able to sort out the items needed for different orders so I can keep everything together.

I try my best not to pet and rub the supplies like I would a puppy in need of attention, but there are times I find myself letting fabric run through my fingers as I think of exactly how to use it to its highest potential. It's hard to fight the urge to start on a few projects while there's still so much disarray in the room.

I'm elbows deep in a box of thread when a throat clears at the doorway.

I smile instantly as I turn to look in that direction.

"That is a hit to my ego," Oracle says as he steps inside. "I don't think I've seen someone stop smiling so fast in my life."

"Sorry," I say.

"Either you're wishing I wasn't here, or you're wishing I was someone else."

I turn my attention back to my task of picking between the two, but he's right. I'm a little disappointed he isn't Emmett. At least that's who immediately came to mind when he approached.

"I can handle it," he says. "At least I think I can. Do you need some help?"

I do, but Em said that Emmett was going to work on the furniture.

"I think I need to do it so I know where everything ends up," I explain, not wanting to shoo him out of here, but the thought of misplacing something causes me more stress. I don't have an unlimited budget, and if I have to replace something, it cuts into my profit. Since I'm working off favors, that's still sitting at zero until the football order is complete.

"I won't touch your supplies," he says, pulling one of the furniture boxes away from the wall so he can get a better look at the finished product on the front.

He's not pushy with his presence, and I have to consider he's almost as new here as I am. Maybe he's just wanting a familiar face among all the new ones like I did when I wanted to be around Emmett. Who am I kidding, familiarity is one of the things I was less interested in when my thoughts drifted to that man.

"I can work on this," he offers.

I want to refuse, but hell, he's here and Emmett isn't. If he puts the sewing desk together, I'm one step closer to getting my machine out of the bedroom and in here so I can actually start on one of my orders.

"That would be great," I tell him. "I think I want it on that wall over there."

He nods before pulling some type of multi-tool from his pocket and flipping out a knife to slice at the tape holding the box closed.

"Handy," I say as I watch him work.

He winks at me, making me realize just how handsome he is. I know I should probably date this guy. He's quick to smile. There's less baggage where he's concerned. He doesn't seem like he feels the need to fight his attraction to me like it's some sort of sin the way Emmett does. But even as handsome as he is, I don't feel an ounce of the chemistry that I feel with Emmett.

I must stare too long because Oracle stops what he's doing and looks back in my direction.

"What is it?"

"You don't seem like the type of guy who dates," I blurt, my eyes going wide because honestly, I didn't mean to say my thoughts out loud.

A frown tugs down the corners of his mouth. "I don't date."

I guess it's commendable that he doesn't lie and add that he'd change that for me, knowing he honestly wouldn't.

After all, he did *predict* that he could see my clothes on his bedroom floor. He didn't ask me out to dinner or tell me he could see any kind of future with me.

"If I gave you that impression—"

I hold up my hand to halt his words. "You didn't. I think—"

"I have to take this," he says without even looking when his phone rings in his pocket.

He looks as relieved as I feel when he rushes out of the room.

I blow out a breath, trying to shove down the awkwardness I'm feeling.

I don't know that I've ever seen someone run away, scared of me. I chuckle, recalling the terrified look in his eyes as he bolted from the room.

20

LEGACY

Something unfamiliar seeps into my veins when I see Oracle emerge from the mouth of the hallway. I don't even know the guy. I haven't shared a word of conversation with him other than the look he gave me yesterday evening, but I'm still fighting the urge to punch him in the nose for just existing and stepping into Devyn's orbit as he walks closer.

He pulls his phone from his ear. "Devyn is putting her room together. She probably needs help assembling some of the furniture."

He walks away before I can speak, making me wonder what call would be so important that he'd leave that woman alone.

I'm feeling a little disappointed that I wasn't there when she found out about the room being provided for her business. I tried my best as I carried in a slew of boxes earlier, to organize them by attempting to guess what was in them according to their labels, but I'm sure she has a different method than the one I used.

I walk, despite wanting to run, in that direction. My desperation to see her is what carried me outside for a long jog up the street and back. I'm full of all of this unspent energy, and the urges I feel when it comes to her need to settle some before I do something we both might regret.

"What's so funny?" I ask, hearing her laughter from the doorway.

She jerks her head in my direction, and God help me for the way her eyes home in on the dampness on my shirt.

"He freaked out when I asked if he was the type of guy who dated."

Her response grabs every ounce of my attention.

"Is that what we're doing? Dating other people?"

She slowly shakes her head.

"I blurted a thought, and it freaked him out."

"You were thinking about dating him?"

"Would you stop overanalyzing every word?"

I step closer into the room. "What else would you have me do?"

I have a list a mile long if she's looking for suggestions.

She points her finger across the room to where I gathered all the things that need to be assembled.

"Is that all you want from me?" I tease. "Furniture assembly?"

She shakes her head, a slow back-and-forth movement as her eyes once again wander down my body.

I turn my back to her, because there would be too much to explain if I keep facing her.

The laughter from her side of the room tells me she isn't as inexperienced as I originally thought since it seems she can read me like a book.

"How long do you plan on working?" I ask as I rip open the first box.

"Until it's done."

I look around the room. Em told me this isn't even half of what she has coming in, and I've already worked out a plan with Kincaid for when her new machine arrives.

"I'll help where I can," I tell her.

I do my best to keep my attention on my task at hand as I spread out the pieces according to the instructions, but I lose focus every time even the slightest noise comes from her. She's meticulous as she organizes her supplies. She reads every piece of paper that comes in the box, forming a pile and muttering something about *needing a filing cabinet for shit like this.*

I can only keep half my mind on my own task because I'm waiting to see what she does next. I see her get distracted as if she wishes all of this work was done and she could jump to the fun part. I know I'm focusing on her maturity because there's a part of me that needs her to not be the typical eighteen-year-old. If she was all giggly and boy crazy and said things like OMG! I could never take her seriously, and there would be no chance of anything between us.

I know I'm looking for something that will make me pump the brakes, but she just keeps on working, her eyes lighting up with every package she opens as if it's Christmas morning and someone shopped her wish list to the letter.

She's in sweats and a bulky sweater, her messy hair pinned haphazardly to the top of her head, and there's just something about the whole package that I find irresistible. She didn't try to straighten her clothes or fix her hair when I entered, and I highly doubt she did it for Oracle when he was in here earlier either. She's unapologetically her, and there's just something insanely sexy about that.

"So, you talked to Oracle about dating?" I ask, trying for casual and somehow managing to sound anything but.

She chuckles. "You just can't let it go, can you? He said he doesn't date. Do you date?"

"I said I wanted to take you out."

"Before me, did you date?"

I shake my head, honesty being my only choice where she's concerned.

"So you just hookup?"

The screws I'm counting out become very interesting all of a sudden.

"Emmett?"

I look up at her. "I'm not talking to you about sex."

"We're going to be dating. It shouldn't make you uncomfortable."

"I'm not uncomfortable," I say, lying despite telling myself I wouldn't.

"If we're going to date, we need to be able to have these conversations. Isn't date three the date we get down and dirty?"

I shake my head at the same time my cock thickens in my athletic shorts. Jesus, why didn't I pull on jeans before coming in here?

"Down and dirty, as you put it, happens when two people are ready," I correct.

"You're looking ready."

I snap my eyes up to hers, wanting to tug that damn lip clamped between her teeth free with my own.

"You need to stop."

"What if I'm ready before the first date?" she challenges.

My mind doesn't give a shit that she's in baggy clothes. My memory is great, and I know exactly what her bare legs look like in a dress. Heat flares inside of me when she shifts her weight from one foot to the other, like she suddenly wants to clamp her thighs together. The sacrifices I would make to have my head there when she does.

"You won't be," I growl, the words a warning that for some reason I'm also praying she will challenge.

"Have you had one-night stands?"

I take a ragged deep breath.

"What?"

"Have you—"

"Stop. Just don't," I interrupt.

She chuckles, but then her face falls. My mind races with the possibilities.

"Have you?"

She swallows. "I didn't know that's what it was going to be."

"I'll kill him."

She shakes her head, a derisive sound falling from her perfect lips. "He's not worth the jail time. Seb isn't a bad guy. He's just not mature enough to stick around and have a hard conversation. He told me it was a mistake and scurried away. He probably thinks he was doing me a favor by not having to tell me he wasn't interested in more with me. It's likely he thought that he was protecting my feelings for not rejecting me to my face. It took me a really long time to finally accept that everything that happened had more to do with his shortcomings than mine."

"That explanation makes me want to hurt him even more," I grumble. "What did you say his last name was?"

She snorts a laugh, and I let her pretend that I wasn't being serious.

21

Devyn

I smile down at the adorable appliqued polar bear Alyssa chose for the matching pajamas, using a pair of angled scissors to snip a few threads. I'm glad every shirt is designed with the same image. It makes it less likely that I'll make a mistake, considering that I can't keep my mind on my work.

It's been a week since I told Emmett about Seb. A week of him stopping by to visit. A week of him keeping his distance regardless of how jealous I interpreted him to be. A week of him watching my mouth when I speak but never getting close enough for us to kiss again.

I'm all for slow burn in a romance novel, but in real life, I want the warmth of his skin against my fingertips. I want his hands tangled in my hair. I want the hardness of every inch of his body pressed to mine.

I want—The scissors fall from my hand, clattering on the tabletop.

I'm exactly what he accused high school boys of being—horny.

I've gotten all googly-eyed over a guy before. It's hard to be in the middle of a group of people all revved up for sex and not be affected somehow by the pheromones. Plus, it's like a rite of passage to have a crush on someone, to write their name in a notebook with little hearts. I've experienced that, but I've never thought about stripping them naked and doing things I've only ever seen while searching X-rated websites when boredom strikes late at night. There had been times when I wondered if I even had a sex drive because getting down and dirty with someone is rarely where my head goes, and even less after that night with Seb.

"Is this a bad time?"

I turn toward the feminine voice and smile.

"This is a perfect time," I tell Khloe as she steps into the room.

The excitement in her eyes as she looks across the room to the bag hanging there matches my own.

"When I tell you this stressed me out," I say as I walk toward the bag.

"I didn't mean to cause you stress," she says, her face falling a little.

"No, no," I insist. "In the best way possible. I'm honored you trusted me with this, but I won't lie and say I wasn't nervous. I was terrified to mess it up."

I tug down the zipper, but her hands rush up to her face, covering her mouth before I get it fully unwrapped.

"That's my dress?" she asks from behind her hands.

My pulse immediately quickens. "Oh God."

She shakes her head. "No, not like that. It's beautiful."

"Really?" I read her the wrong way, and it will take a moment to get over that rush of failure that hit me immediately.

"I love it," Khloe says, reaching out and letting some of the tulle slide between her fingers.

"You should try it on, so I can make sure the fit is perfect."

I hand her the hanger, grinning at the extra pep in her walk as she heads to the bathroom.

"I think this is what you've been waiting for."

Seeing Emmett always brings a rush of excitement, but the huge box in his arms is the real winner today.

"The footballs!"

This shipment has been delayed more than once. I haven't wasted my time. I've been able to complete other orders while waiting, but this order is what set everything in motion, and I've been eager to get started on it.

"There's more than one," he says as he places the box against the far wall. "I'll carry them all in."

I thank him, but then my attention is pulled back to Khloe as she steps out of the bathroom with tears in her eyes.

"Wow. You're stunning."

She pushes a hand against her hair as if she struggles with compliments.

"I feel as beautiful as I did the day I got married."

I watch as she turns in front of the mirror, checking every angle.

It's no longer white. She wanted it dyed a burgundy color. Originally, it swept the floor, but now it teases the tops of her knees. The sequins didn't take the dye, but their opal coloring, something I was initially worried about, are magnificent in their contrast, looking like dew drops on the bodice.

"Thank you," she whispers.

"Think Kid will like it?"

"He's going to love it," she assures me, taking one final look at herself in the mirror before heading back into the bathroom to change.

Her anniversary isn't until spring, so there will be a few more months before she'll be able to show off my hard work, but I know it's going to be well worth the wait.

"I was thinking," I tell her as she exits with the dress back in the protective bag. "Would you be interested in a mini photoshoot with it? I was hoping to use it for my portfolio."

Her eyes widen with excitement. "That would be amazing."

We chat for a little while longer before she insists I get back to work. Emmett comes and goes four more times with boxes of footballs, and I realize as I start to run out of room, that I underestimated how much space so many balls would take up.

"What's that about?" he asks, coming in with yet another box.

"What's that?" I ask, my hands working on pulling back the tape on one of the boxes.

"The longest sigh I've ever heard," he answers.

"These boxes were delayed," I mutter. "I'm behind."

"You have time. Didn't the guy say he didn't need them until closer to Thanksgiving?"

"Yes, but I have a million other orders. The pajamas for example."

"The Polar Express thing isn't until the week of Christmas," he says, his hand covering mine on the box. "Look at me."

I swallow as I look up at him. "I think it's more work than I can do."

The confession is difficult to make out loud even though it's been floating in my head since I was able to sit down at my machine in this room for the first time. Yet, I've still taken more orders since then.

"I can help. There are others who can help."

"I need to do this on my own."

"You need to be able to admit when you're drowning. There's no shame in needing help."

"I—"

My eyes flutter closed when his palm lifts to my face.

"We can get the balls ready to go in no time."

"It's not just getting them on the machine," I explain. "I didn't take into consideration the time it takes to cut them open, create each individual file, run the program, and then stitch them all back together. Just the file creation alone is going to take several days."

"Leave that part with me," he says, pulling out his phone and firing off a text before shoving it back into his front pocket.

"It's still going to take forever." I hate how whiny my voice sounds. I hate it even more that I sound like a kid complaining rather than a business owner who needs to search for a solution.

"It can't take forever," he says as he steps back. "You owe me a date when it's done, remember?"

It feels like he's offering me a reward of sorts, a bonus for completing a job, and I love the sound of it.

"I'll be thirty myself by then. My obligation is to my backers and clients."

"That's very mature."

He steps even closer, and I start to wonder if a ten-minute break, one filled with our lips locked together and hands roaming, isn't such a bad thing.

All I get, however, is a brush of his lips before a throat clears near the door.

I want to stomp my damn foot.

"You needed me?"

I look around Emmett to see Max standing there.

"Yeah," Emmett says. "I was hoping you could help us with something."

22

LEGACY

"What's going on?" Devyn asks as she takes a cautious step into the room.

"We're working," Oracle explains, holding the seam ripper up for her to see.

She doesn't look relieved. She looks terrified as if she's worried we're in here sabotaging her and setting her back further than she was when she went to bed only a few hours ago. I stayed here with her the entire time helping her, but it became very clear very quickly that she was right. She was underwater, and although she technically has time to do this all on her own, the amount of work she's facing would end up leaving her disheartened. I've told myself over and over I'm helping her, but honestly, I'm growing anxious for that damn date. I wanted it to take a long time, but I'm finding that I'm actually a little impatient about it. The sooner she can knock this order out, the easier it will be for me to convince her to take an evening off and have dinner with me.

I grin at Oracle. The man was so willing to help, but I get the feeling that he no longer has his sights set on her. I don't know if the dating question made him change his mind or if he's a better guy than I originally assumed and he's stepping out of the way for me. I can say with a hundred percent certainty that she deserves better than him because he's been here a week or so and I've already seen him having breakfast with two different conquests before he sent them on their way.

Instead of staying across the room, I approach her, brushing a kiss on her lips, half because I can't resist and half because I don't want Oracle changing his mind.

She blinks up at me when I take a step back, that sexy pink tongue of hers licking at the taste of my lips left behind.

"How did you sleep?"

"Alone," she says, the words soft and absent as if she didn't mean to say it out loud.

"That's good to hear," I say, knowing there's a very slim chance Kincaid would let anyone in his house even if she had options. Hell, I wouldn't take that chance.

"Would've been better if you were there."

It wouldn't take much for me to get completely lost in this woman. Just the sight of her turns me on more than any other woman who came before her. I open my mouth to tell her she's wrong. If I were in bed with her, the last thing that would happen would be sleep.

"I can't concentrate with all these pheromones floating through the air," Oracle says, laughter in his tone.

Her cheeks heat, pinkness crawling up her throat, making me wonder what a flush from an orgasm would look like on her perfect skin.

"Let's get to work," I tell her, more for my benefit than hers.

I'm not feeling any more in control of myself than I accused those teenage boys she mentioned of being right now. I find that I like the chaos swarming in my gut. It makes me feel alive and a little reckless.

"What's first on your agenda this morning, Ms. Malloy?"

She grins, looking up at me, but Oracle clears his throat again. I lift my gaze, a warning making my eyes squint. I'll hurt him for being such a damn cockblock.

She lifts the laptop she has under her arm.

"I have to do all of those files," she says, and I've been waiting for this moment.

"I have them right here," I tell her, pulling a slim jump drive from my pocket.

I feel like a hero when her eyes widen. "Really?"

"Max said it took about ten minutes. He has some kind of sorting program that was able to populate the entire list."

She blinks down at the jump drive, her chin starting to quiver.

"Hey," I say, stepping in closer to her. "What's all that about?"

She shakes her head. "I've just been stressing over getting it done."

"Well, you have people here to help, so use us how you need us."

"That sounds like a great idea," Oracle says, like he pulled the words right out of my head.

He chuckles when I glare at him again. I don't get the vibe he's actually going to try and hook up with Devyn, but I know he's going to fuck with me the entire time.

"This saves me at least a day or two of work," she says as she sets her computer on the table and takes the drive from my hand. "I'll have to do something special to thank him."

"I've been cutting apart these footballs," Oracle reminds her. "Are you taking requests?"

She chuckles, paying him no real attention either as she plugs the drive into her machine.

"He did them in batches of two." She looks back at me with an even wider smile on her face. "I can run two at the same time. That literally cuts my processing time in half."

"Max said he'll show you how to do it for the baseball order."

"Don't jinx me. I haven't gotten that order yet. It hasn't even been discussed."

"You'll get it," I guarantee.

Her eyes search mine for something, and it makes me wonder how many times she's been disappointed in her life that she's wary of every good thing that happens to her. It's a sad sort of existence honestly, to always question someone's intention and if they're being genuine.

We get to work. Even when the first couple of footballs aren't up to her standard, she stays focused, explaining that she planned for a few mistakes and ordered extra footballs.

By the time we're on the third team of balls, we have a system down. Oracle is cutting balls apart, placing all the treads he cuts away in the trash after she mentioned the mess he was making. I'm trimming the threads that the machine places between each letter. It isn't the easiest job considering how tiny the scissors are and how big my damn fingers are, but I'd never complain. I'm in her orbit, and for some reason, it's my happy place right now. She's loading the machine, making sure that it's positioned perfectly and pulling the printed balls off when it's done.

"I hope you guys are good with a needle because it's going to take a year to sew these things up," she mutters under her breath, looking at the table loaded down with the printed balls.

"So long as we're done by next week," Oracle quickly agrees. "I don't want to miss the trip to Denver."

I swear I'll strangle the guy for bringing that shit up in front of her.

Her eyes widen, excitement making them sparkle. "Denver?"

I swallow, keeping my eyes on my work.

"You want to go?"

I snap my eyes up at him.

"There's a fabric store there I wanted to visit. Think I could tag along?"

"No," I snap just as Oracle declares, "That would be great."

Her head swivels twice, looking from me to him and then back to me.

"You're supposed to take me places," she says cautiously, and the hint of irritation in her voice does things to my body that I like a little too much.

"Any place she wants to go," Oracle adds. "I'm sure she'd like to go to Hale-ish."

"I swear," I growl in warning but the guy only laughs.

"What's Hale-ish? The fabric store I want to go to is called Sew Delicious. They have a café there as well, which at first seems like a bad idea, you know? To mix fabric and food, but it really works for them, and I think—"

"It's a sex club." Oracle interrupts.

Her head snaps so quickly in his direction I worry about her neck hurting.

"A wh-what?"

"Sex club," Oracle says, his eyes on the seam ripper he's using to cut apart the footballs. "You know, dark rooms, public sex, and orgasms."

"I've never been," I say, needing her to know that although I don't see an issue with what others do, that place really isn't my thing. "I wasn't planning on going."

"You got a gift card," Oracle says as if that gift requires I use it.

"It sounds like fun," Devyn says.

"Really?" I don't bother to try and hide the surprise in my voice.

I have no claim on this woman. What happens if she goes and finds someone there to hook up with? The idea of getting arrested for beating the shit out of someone at the club rushes through my head. I know it would happen too. There's no scenario where I'd sit back and watch Devyn mess around with someone else despite her having every right to choose who she wants to mess around with.

"I've read about places like that," she continues, her eyes on her work as if she's speaking about something as simple as the weather. The tremble in her hands tells me that she's nervous to speak about these things.

I point my tiny scissors at Oracle in warning when he opens his mouth to speak again.

When neither of us respond, she drops the subject, but I don't feel relieved. I know the conversation isn't over.

An hour later, Oracle declares that he's done. When Devyn tells him there's nothing else that he can help with right now, he leaves the room.

I know my luck has run out when she pulls two balls off the machine and looks up at me rather than readying another pair to be embroidered.

"Why don't you want me to go with you to that club?"

"I wasn't going to that club in the first place," I explain. I might've gone before she showed up here, but there's no way I'd go now. There isn't an ounce of thrill for me when I think about it.

I can tell she wants to talk about it, but her cheeks are also flaming with color. I don't want her to feel uncomfortable discussing anything with me, so instead of shutting the conversation down, I let her take the lead.

"Do you want to go?"

She shrugs. "I want to experience things."

"Public sex?" I ask before I can stop myself.

If she says yes, I may have to come to terms with the fact that we aren't compatible at all. I've never been turned on by the idea of people watching me have sex, and the thought of getting down and dirty with Devyn while in front of an audience makes me want to claw people's eyes out. It makes me feel territorial and possessive in the most animalistic and feral ways.

"I don't think so," she says, her nose scrunching up. "What about you?"

I shake my head. "Nope. I don't like to share, not even watching."

Her teeth dig into her lower lip as she tries to hide a smile.

"You still want to go, don't you?"

"I want to go to that fabric store, too," she adds.

This woman is going to drive me insane.

"If anyone touches you, I'll have to kill them. You know that, right?"

"I'll make sure I stick to your side the entire time," she promises.

"Good girl," I say absently, but my cock threatens to come to life when she smiles even wider.

23

Devyn

"I love your excitement," Emmett says as he pulls out of the bank parking lot.

"This makes everything official," I say, spreading my finger on top of the folder on my lap.

"Can I say how proud I am of you without it sounding condescending?"

"Of course," I answer. "I'm pretty proud of myself."

"You should be. Few people your age have the focus and drive that you have."

My smile falls a little. I know my age is a huge issue for him, and I feel like no matter how many times we move forward, every time he mentions it, we move back a few paces.

"I've always been mature for my age," I remind him, saying the same words I've said every time he mentions it.

Honestly, I'm starting to grow weary of the reminders. I keep my mouth shut because I know this is something he's trying to work through, and it's not my place to rush that along for him.

I turn my gaze out the window. It has been a huge day for me. I finished the football order and Emmett took me to drop them off. The coach was ecstatic about them, and right there in the parking lot of the high school, offered the baseball job to me. I gladly took it of course even though embroidering on sports equipment isn't exactly going in the direction I want to take my business. I'd be a fool to turn it down.

With the paperwork from Max creating my LLC, I was able to open a business bank account and deposit the final payment. I've never had that much money in all my life. As Emmett drives, I resist the urge to pull up my banking app and stare at the balance.

"Where are we going?" I ask when he doesn't take the road that will lead us back to the clubhouse.

"Lunch."

"I'm not exactly dressed for a date," I say, waiting for him to deny that's what this will be.

I know it's not exactly mature to test him this way, but it's always hot and cold with him. He'll brush his lips against mine, but I haven't felt the sweep of his tongue since that very first time he kissed me. I crave that from him. When he mentioned taking things slowly, I had no idea he meant that the continents would shift on their tectonic plates faster.

"You always look beautiful," he says rather than arguing.

As he continues to drive, I busy myself with tangling my fingers together. I know what I want to talk about, but I can't seem to garner the courage to bring the sex club back up. I overheard several of the guys talking about it yesterday because the day they picked is tomorrow. Emmett hasn't brought it up either, making me think he has no interest in going. Either that or he wants to go alone. The thought makes my stomach sour, and I doubt I'll be able to eat anything because of it.

"Do you like Italian?" he asks, pulling up to a small, locally owned bistro. "This place is new. I haven't tried it yet. There's a new steakhouse out on the highway too, if this doesn't interest you."

"This looks great." I attempt a smile, but the idea that he'll go to Denver with his friends and hookup with someone else saddens me. I find myself struggling to hide it.

"What's wrong?"

I shake my head. "Nothing. It's just been a busy day already."

I wasn't joking about being underdressed. When we step inside we are welcomed by a man in a suit and a tie.

Emmett doesn't appear at all out of place despite his jeans and leather vest. My body lights on fire when he guides me through the restaurant with his hand on my hip. I don't get a moment of reprieve when he chooses to sit beside me rather than across from me, despite the host placing the menus on opposite sides of the table.

"Your server Courtney will be with you shortly," the host says before walking away.

"He thought I was your dad or something," Emmett mutters as he reaches for his menu on the far side of the table.

"He didn't," I argue.

"Then he's an asshole because his eyes did a full-body scan the second you walked inside. Not that I can blame the guy. You look edible today."

I swallow down a grin, my lips still tugging up in the corner.

"So you claim me in front of some guy who doesn't matter, but you won't do it at the clubhouse in front of the guys you work with."

He shifts, his thigh rubbing against mine, and I swear I see arcs of electricity sparking between our bodies.

"I don't have to claim you at the clubhouse, Devyn. Everyone there already knows you're mine."

I tilt my head to the side, unwilling to let his words sink too deep inside. This is freaking news to me.

"Yours?" I argue. "How is that possible when you won't even kiss me?"

In that same frustrating way he does when he first sees me and then again when we part ways for the evening, he leans in, brushing his lips against mine and pulling back before I can take it further.

"I kiss you all the time," he says, his words low, meant for only me to hear.

A frustrated growl leaves my lips when he grins. He knows exactly what he's doing.

"Can I interest you in a glass of wine or a draft beer?"

I feel like a queen when he's slow to pull his eyes from mine before looking up at the waitress.

"She's not—"

"Water with lemon, please," I say before he can let the world know I'm not old enough to drink.

"I'll have the same," he says, his cheek twitching as if he knows exactly what I just did.

"Any appetizers?"

"We need a little time to look at the menu," Emmett tells her with a smile.

Despite her walking up to us almost kissing, she still looks at him like she has a chance.

"Are you flirting with the waitress right in front of me?"

His eyes snap to mine. "No, Devyn. I'd never disrespect you like that."

"Because I'm sitting right here?"

"Even if you weren't," he declares. "I'm not that kind of guy."

"So you aren't going to hook up with someone else tomorrow night?"

"Tomorrow night?"

"The guys are going to the club. I presumed you were going with them, seeing as you have a gift card and all." Even using all my might, I still can't manage to keep the bitterness out of my tone.

"I figured you were going to go, too."

This news shocks me. We haven't mentioned the club since that first day.

"You want me to go?"

"I'd prefer not to go at all, but I'm not going to stop you."

"You want to hook up with me at the club?"

He shakes his head immediately. "I don't want what's going on between us to start in a sex club."

"There are over twenty-four hours between then and now," I say, my cheeks warming with the suggestion. "A lot can happen between us in that amount of time."

"Devyn," he groans, shifting in his seat.

"You always do that," I complain, dropping my eyes to the menu in my hands but finding myself incapable of deciphering the words. My mind is racing with all the possibilities, some of them not good at all.

"Do what?"

"Shut me down. I feel like sometimes you wish I were someone else, or that you want to do some things, but just not with me."

He turns toward me, his body shifting against my side. Gently, he turns my head, forcing me to look at him.

"Did you miss the fact that I just called you mine?"

I swallow, my lips parting the slightest bit. "But you don't want to—"

"Oh, sweetheart. Do I ever want to, but I'm not going to rush this. I refuse to let carnal urges force my hand. We have to make sure this is right, that it's something we both want. I can't risk hurting you."

I nod, understanding what he means. I'm more than ready and have been for quite some time, but it's not fair for me to rush him either. I'm sure I could tempt him. I could use coercion to force him into action, but he could end up regretting what we do, and that's the very last thing I want to happen.

Courtney comes back with our drinks, and the spell is temporarily broken. We order our food, and chat about the orders I'll be working on for the next couple of days as we wait.

My body hums the entire time, my fingers wanting to roam over his skin, but I manage to keep my hands to myself.

It doesn't stop the hum in my body that's making my skin itch.

By the time we make it back to the clubhouse, I'm on fire. I know I need to go back inside and get to work, but I slide past Emmett when he opens the passenger door for me and start to walk around the side of the clubhouse. There's no privacy inside, and I already feel like the Cerberus members can read every thought that swims through my head.

He has done absolutely nothing out of the ordinary to set me on fire, but that hasn't stopped the flames of arousal from licking at my skin since he declared me his.

My hands are trembling as we round the corner of the clubhouse. It isn't exactly a hundred percent private. With the positioning of Misty's house, anyone looking out the bedroom window on the second floor could see us, but it's the best option right now.

I stop in my tracks, loving the way his arm immediately wraps around my waist so he doesn't knock me over.

"What's wrong?" he asks as I turn toward him.

I shake my head, lifting on my toes and pressing my mouth to his.

"Dev—"

I slip my tongue inside his mouth before he can protest, and much to my surprise, he grips me tighter. My insides come alive, my belly flipping over as tingles race all over my body. It gives a whole new meaning to butterflies.

He holds me tighter as he guides me against the building, the bricks warm from the afternoon sun.

I cling to him, knowing this won't last long. He'll come to his senses and pull away soon.

I feel the groan that rumbles out of him in my bones. When he pushes against me, I no longer have any doubts about how much this man wants me. I feel it in every hard inch of him. I press harder against him, my hand releasing his shirt to run along his side.

He breaks the kiss. His breathing has changed as much as mine has, and he grabs my hand before I can sweep it down the front of his jeans.

"Devyn," he says. "Don't."

I blink up at him, confused. We both want the same thing. I just can't wrap my head around him always hitting the brakes.

"You don't want me."

He huffs a humorless laugh. "I couldn't stop wanting you if I tried, but that's not all this is."

"You want more?" I know the question is a risk. He could easily reject me with his next breath.

"So much more," he says.

I'm both elated and annoyed when cool air replaces his warmth as he steps back.

24

LEGACY

I know I've done some bad things in my life. I've made wrong choices and more mistakes than I could ever count. I knew I was lucky each and every time something went my way, surprised my luck hadn't run out yet.

It ended today.

The kiss I shared with Devyn still burns inside of me, and she's stoking that fire with every move she makes around this damn sewing room of hers.

She went to Em and Kincaid's house and came back wearing what I imagine is the shortest damn dress she owns.

I came close to coming in my jeans when I asked why she changed and she informed me that I turned her on so much she ruined her other clothes. As if the idea of her arousal coating her skin wasn't enough of a tease, she seems hell-bent to keep me turned on with every move. The fluttery dress teases the back of her thighs. I swear I see the curvature of her ass cheeks more than once when she bends over to pull supplies out of the lowest bin on the cubicle shelf I assembled for her.

"You don't even need that right now," I say, calling her out because she's more than a little obvious about what she's doing at this point.

"You don't seem to mind," she says, taking her time to put the items back in the bin before standing up straight.

I don't rush to pull my gaze from her legs as she turns around to face me.

I told her we needed to wait, but she's chipping away at that resolve every second we spend together.

She has to know that getting to know each other is a must, but we're both in trouble because the chemistry between us feels like a physical thing that could be bottled up and sold.

"My attraction to you isn't in question."

"I can tell," she says, her eyes dropping to the front of my jeans.

I grip myself over the denim, making her breath catch in her throat. I simply readjust myself, trying to ease the discomfort I'm feeling.

"Emmett," she whispers, taking a step in my direction.

I swear if she touches me, I'll lock the goddamned door and make her scream my name. We can even cuddle after so she doesn't feel used.

My eyes scan the room, trying to figure out the best place for all of this to take place. I wouldn't want to ruin anything and set her back.

"Is this a bad time?"

"Yes," Devyn says to Oracle, making him laugh.

"No," I argue. "It's not. What's up?"

"We're figuring out transportation, so we need a final head count. Are you two going tomorrow?"

"No," I say.

"To Denver?" Devyn asks.

"Yes," Oracle says.

"No," I repeat.

"Yes," Devyn argues, her eyes locked on my face. "Can we also stop by Sew Delicious?"

"Of course," Oracle says. "Are they open on Sundays?"

"They are," Devyn says, excitement in her voice.

"I'll take you to the fabric store. We don't have to go to—"

"What should I wear?" she asks, ignoring my insistence that going to Hale-ish won't happen.

I take a step forward when Oracle's eyes dip to the very short hem of Devyn's dress.

"That would work," Oracle praises.

Oracle chuckles when I inch even closer, holding his hands up in mock surrender.

"So territorial," he mutters, taking a step back. "But I don't blame you one bit."

"Emmett?" Devyn's voice has a hint of pleading in it. I like the idea that she's wanting me to agree to going rather than arguing that she'll go whether I do or not.

I look in her direction, knowing how impossibly hard it will be to keep my cool if anyone there tries to hit on her.

"We'll go," I say eventually, earning a little squeal from Devyn that my body reads in ways it shouldn't while in mixed company.

"Remember, it's an overnight trip," Oracle says as he turns toward the door. "I'll book your hotel room when I book the others."

"Rooms," I clarify. "Plural. We aren't going to share a room."

"Really?" both Devyn and Oracle ask at the same time.

I confirm. Devyn looks disappointed. Oracle looks like he doesn't believe me one bit.

"Make sure Em and Kincaid know you'll be gone," Oracle says before leaving the room.

"Oh God," she says the second he's gone. "I can't have that conversation with them."

I chuckle. "Part of being an adult is not being embarrassed when you're doing adult things."

She narrows her eyes at me. "Will you ever get past the age thing?"

"Maybe when you're forty," I mutter. "What were we doing before he showed up?"

"You were staring at my legs with an erection."

She laughs when I swallow, fighting the urge to drop my eyes to her bare skin once again.

"I have to go," I rush out, knowing if I stay, the thoughts I had earlier, very well may come to fruition.

"See you later." It sounds like a challenge as if she can read me and knows I have no ability to walk away from her.

"You're driving me insane."

"Seems only fair." She takes several steps closer to me. As much as I know I should take a step back, I'm locked in place.

To say I'm attracted to her physically is an understatement. I can't get the woman off my mind even when I'm sleeping. She infiltrates damn near every thought while I'm awake and shows up regularly in my dreams.

I have to wonder if it's her connection to Vaughn, and that loss I still feel all these years later is why I seem to be clinging to the idea of us together, but I know it's more than that. Devyn just has something about her that makes men stop and take notice, and it's more than her looks.

I can't count the number of times I've pictured her in my future. It's almost enough to scare me away because those thoughts have never crossed my mind. I was never the type of man to consider a wife and kids. I never wanted to get close to someone enough that losing them would hurt me the way it has in the past. I've never gotten close to friends or any of the women I've been with in the past. Devyn seems to have the uncanny ability to change all of that for me, and that's what makes her so damn dangerous. I want to pull her to me and shove her away all at the same time. My luck is sure to change, and I can't imagine losing her. We've only been around each other for a couple of weeks. She'd be impossible to get over now, not to mention how hard that loss would be if we spent a lengthy amount of time together.

"I thought you were leaving," she says, her body so close to mine, I swear I can feel the heat from her skin.

"I need to," I whisper, dropping my hand to her hip when she steps in even closer.

When her lips brush my neck, I know fighting it any longer would be an absolute waste of time.

I reach up, tangling my hand in her hair. The gasp that escapes her lips makes me rock hard.

"You'll ruin another pair of panties," I warn.

She licks her lips before speaking. "I'm not wearing any."

My mouth hangs open in shock, my cock jerking from need in my jeans.

"You're so fucking naughty," I growl, pressing my lips to her cheek before stepping back.

"You're a tease," she groans, her arms dropping to her sides. "Will we ever fuck?"

That filthy word on her pretty pink lips is almost too much.

I shake my head. "I'll never fuck you, Devyn."

Her face falls as if someone just told her Santa doesn't exist for the very first time.

"No matter how rough I get with you, it'll never be fucking."

She swallows, her throat working as she realizes what I'm promising.

I turn and walk out of the room, her laughter tickling my back when I reach down and readjust myself again.

I find several of the guys in the garage when I enter, needing a little time away from her before I forget all the reasoning of taking it slow with her.

"He looks like he needs to get away too," Stormy says, pointing in my direction as I cross the room to grab a beer.

"Where are you going?" I ask. I haven't heard news of a new job, and since our team was one of the ones to go out last time, there's an unlikely chance that we'll get to go out on the very next one.

"My little brother is getting married," Jinx says. "I was told there was an open invitation to Cerberus for anyone who wanted to attend."

"I think your sister wants Cerberus there," Rocker says, hinting that his sister may have the hots for men in leather cuts.

Jinx shakes his head, but there's no mirth on his face.

"I think all the shit that went down with Cortez and the abductions are the reasons for the invite. They figure with us there, everything will be safer," Jinx says.

"Cortez?" Newton asks.

Jinx proceeds to tell the three new guys what happened in Lindell, Texas, his hometown, in the last year. He goes over the abductions and Angel Guerra's role in all of it.

"Cortez has been neutralized," I remind him.

"The town is still pretty shook up about it," Jinx says.

"I'll go," I volunteer. No one's special day should be ruined by fear, despite the world we live in today.

Several of the other guys also volunteer.

"It's in a couple weeks," Jinx says. "I'll cover the cost of tickets."

"If enough people agree to go, I'm sure Kincaid would let us use the jet," Rocker says as he lifts his beer to his lips.

I take a drink of mine too. I know I'm well and truly fucked when I can't decide if I'll be able to stay away from Devyn, even for only a long weekend.

25

Devyn

I shake out my hands as I wait to the side. I feel like everyone knows why I'm here. It's as if everyone who passes by while Oracle deals with the clerk on grabbing our room keys knows we're going to a sex club later. The lobby would be less busy if we waited until later, but the visit to the club will go well into the night. It just makes more sense to get keys now.

"You don't have to go if you're nervous," Emmett says, his hand settling on my back as he inches closer.

"I want to go," I assure him, knowing my face will flame red the entire time, despite everyone else in attendance being there as well.

I heard from whispering around the clubhouse that there are couples from the MC that come here, but I'm the only female who came tonight. I'm relieved no one else came because I feel like it would be extremely awkward to look them in the eye if I saw anything crazy tonight.

I try to discreetly look over at Stormy, Newton, and Oracle, knowing it's going to be weird regardless.

"We can stay here," Emmett offers. "We don't have to go."

I turn to face him fully, loving the way his eyes always sparkle when he looks at me.

"What do you have in mind?" I ask, my nerves making my voice a little shaky.

"We could order a pizza and watch a movie."

I wait for him to continue, to offer something sexy. The man has the restraint of a priest, and not one of those naughty priests I've read about either. If he doesn't come out and say we're going to mess around, then I know there's a very good chance that we won't. I'm torn between wanting to tempt him into action and also being so quick to pump the brakes because he wants more from me than that.

It didn't take but one kiss for Seb to start pulling at my clothes, but now I know better than to confuse attraction and need with care and affection.

"Maybe if we go," I begin, "you'll be so turned on that you won't be able to shoot me down when we get back."

"I don't pump the brakes because I don't want you, Devyn."

I lift on my toes, letting my fingers get tangled in the suit jacket he's wearing. He doesn't hesitate to press his lips to mine.

"Getting an early start?" Oracle asks, always keen on interrupting us at the worst freaking times.

I sigh in irritation, making Emmett chuckle against my lips.

"You like torturing me," I complain.

"I'm torturing myself, too. Don't forget that."

"Keys," Oracle says. "But I could save a lot of money tonight if you guys just let me watch what you have planned."

Emmett pulls away, positioning himself in front of me.

"You want to explain to the women at Hale-ish why you're bleeding all over them or do you want to give it a rest?"

"Thank you," I say, stepping around Emmett's protective body and taking one of the tiny keycard envelopes from Oracle's hand. "Quit teasing him."

I walk away from both of them, hoping Emmett will follow me. I could easily be persuaded to stay in the hotel, but pizza and a movie is the last thing I want.

Emmett is facing down with Oracle when I climb into the elevator. Oracle is grinning from ear to ear and even takes a moment to wink at me before the doors close. I don't know if his plan is to move Emmett into action, but I'll take all the help I can get.

I don't spend much time in the hotel room. I drop off my suitcase and take a quick look in the mirror. I'm wearing a new dress I recently upcycled. From the way Emmett looked at me when I joined the group in the clubhouse before leaving Farmington, he liked what he saw. Yet, he still somehow managed to keep his hands to himself even though we were all alone in the third-row seat of the SUV for the drive in.

I press a hand to my hair, knowing I don't have time to fix it again before leaving. When I realized Emmett and I weren't going to be making out for the over eight-hour drive, I fell asleep, sinking into the warmth of his arm around my shoulder. I felt safe there. Since I've lost a lot of sleep trying to stay on top of my orders, the rest was welcomed.

All three men are waiting for me in the lobby when I take the elevator back down. Even though there's a part of me that's urging me to take Emmett up on his offer of pizza and a movie, I ignore it and follow them out of the hotel.

"The white, please," I whisper, keeping my eyes on the guy behind the counter rather than looking at Newton, Oracle, and Stormy.

I was going to pick this band color anyway, despite the fact that Emmett chose it too.

I glance at the sign with the descriptions of the bands and what they mean.

Stormy and Oracle got black bands which means they're willing to participate in anything and everything. Newton first said he wanted white but then changed his mind to purple which the signage declares means exhibitionism. I can't decide if that means he likes to watch or likes to be watched.

My cheeks are red, my fingers not wanting to work when the clerk hands me the white band. Emmett pulls it from my fingers and snaps it around my wrist, squeezing my trembling fingers when he finishes.

"We have private rooms if you're interested," the guy behind the counter explains.

"No thank you," Emmett quickly declares.

"It's a great night for new people," the clerk says, not looking the least bit put out at the refusal. He looks in my direction. "Two drink max, but nothing but water, soda, or juice for you."

I nod, wanting to tell him I wouldn't drink even if they let me. I've tasted alcohol before, and I think it's gross.

"Nervous?" Oracle asks, leaning in close as we push through the heavy door on the far side of the room.

"A little," I confess, squeezing Emmett's hand when he takes mine.

"Have fun," Stormy says and like they have a plan in mind, the other three guys split off.

My nervousness settles some with them disappearing into the room, the dim lighting swallowing them up.

"Something to drink?"

I nod. "A water would be great," I tell Emmett, letting him guide me to the bar.

People who walk past us nod, but they don't stop to speak with us. A few guys give me a once-over, but they grin in Emmett's direction like they're complimenting me to him, and I don't know how to feel about it.

A handsome-looking guy with *DYLAN* on his name tag greets us as we step closer to the bar.

"A water and a Coke, please," Emmett says.

"First timers?" Dylan asks as he pulls a cold bottle of water out of a bin and places it on the counter before grabbing a glass for Emmett's Coke.

"Is it that obvious?" I ask.

"Not really. I work every night and remember faces." He slides the Coke across the counter, nodding in appreciation as Emmett stuffs a twenty into the tip jar. "There are monitors all over."

I turn, following the point of Dylan's finger.

"The guys in the bright yellow shirts," he explains. "If you have any issues or feel uncomfortable, just flag one of those guys down. They're here to help and make sure you're having a good time."

"Thanks, man," Emmett says to him before turning to me. "Want to find a seat?"

"Is that what we do, just sit down and watch?"

"People watching is fun," he says, his hand sliding back into mine possessively.

He guides us across the room, picking a dark corner. As we approach, he notices that the area is occupied. As if I've caught someone doing something I shouldn't witness, I jerk my eyes away, quickening my pace when he heads in a different direction.

He leads us to the other corner, and I'm relieved when we see that it's empty.

"She was sucking—"

"I saw what they were doing, Dev. We don't have to discuss it."

I snap my jaw closed, thinking he's in a foul mood but then I see him adjust himself in his slacks before sitting down. He's turned on, and if I let myself think about it, I think I am too.

The air is thick in the club, as if the warmth of everyone breathing and being aroused is settling on my skin as I sit beside him on the small sofa. It's lush and I don't bother resisting rubbing my hands over it, melting into the texture.

"I don't know if tonight was such a good idea," he mutters, snapping his eyes to mine.

I look to my right where his eyes were and gasp. I knew we'd see things tonight. I did a little research on sex clubs when Oracle mentioned it. The research pulled up varying results depending on the location, but the consensus was the same. People would be having sex and would be engaging in various sexual acts all over the place. There would be same-sex interactions, oral sex, and even group sex going on. I thought reading about it would prepare me for it, but as I watch the man on the stage lower his mouth to his partner's private area, the zing of awareness I felt seeing this sort of thing on the computer is nothing like what I'm feeling now.

Emmett clears his throat. "Is that something you like?"

I swallow, trying to ensure I can speak without squeaking. "I wouldn't know."

"Never been tied up?"

I figure I can handle a mature conversation about likes and dislikes.

"Never had umm—" I point to the couple on stage, watching with my mouth hanging open as she wiggles in her restraints, her body convulsing with an apparent orgasm. "That."

"An orgasm?" He sounds the way he did that day that he asked me what Seb's last name was.

"That either," I tell him, turning my head to look at him because the man is now standing and unzipping his jeans.

"No one has ever eaten—"

I press my fingertips to his lips. "No. I don't have a lot of experience, but I'm hoping that doesn't turn you off."

"It doesn't," he assures me. "And I want you to know, that most people would consider me very vanilla. There will be a lot of stuff you might see tonight that I haven't done either."

"What about that?" I say, angling my head back to the couple. "Have you done that?"

He glances up, his eyelids growing heavy. "Yeah. I've done that. Have you?"

I shake my head, my eyes locked on the man as he holds the back of the woman's head, pressing his penis to her lips.

"But I'd like to."

His groan draws the attention of several people across the room.

26

LEGACY

Her eyes stay locked on the couple performing on stage, and I count my blessings that she's witnessing something most would consider pretty straight-laced rather than some whipping scene or group sex.

I'm all about to each their own, but I don't want her thinking that everything she sees is something I might want to do to her. I sure as fuck won't share her. I don't even want the men walking by giving her a cursory glance, much less watching some other man put his hands on her. My breathing increases with the idea.

She shifts in her seat, looking turned on more and more by the second. I know she has to be slick with arousal. My cock aches in my slacks just watching her wiggle. Her eyes dart in my direction several times, but I don't pull my gaze from the side of her face even when her cheeks flame with heat.

There's a sheen of sweat at her temples, and more than once, I've watched a bead of sweat make the path from her throat to that shadow between her breasts. It's taking a lot of strength not to touch her.

The scrape of a chair not far from us draws my attention, and I want to claw the man's eyes out as he looks at her with clear desire in his eyes. I know what he sees. Only unlike me when I first realized my attraction to her, he doesn't look the least bit ashamed for how young she is. Devyn is of age, and for some that's all that matters. But there are still times I try to fight my attraction to her because that whole barely legal thing never appealed to me.

I pull my eyes from the other man, wanting to pull her closer to me, but her attention is locked on the stage where the man is using the ropes of the swing to pull his partner on and off his cock. Her pleasure is palpable, her cries as genuine as the way he holds his mouth open as he fucks her. They may be in the middle of a performance, but there's nothing fake about the way they feel.

"Never in my entire life," she whispers, and I have to nod my head in agreement.

I know watching the couple has its own ability to arouse me, but I think it's more watching her get aroused by it that turns me on the most.

"Did you see them?" I ask, pointing a finger in the direction of a man who has a woman on his lap, a thin blanket covering her waist. Her breasts are exposed, and it's clear that his hand is working her under the blanket as they watch the couple on stage.

As if Devyn can't help herself, she inches even closer, the side of her body touching mine.

"Do you want that?" I ask, knowing my words are a tease because I'd never share her pleasure with anyone, ever. "Do you want my hands on you? In you?"

She looks up at me, her breathing growing a little ragged as she nods.

I suddenly reconsider the offer of one of the private rooms the guy at the counter gave us when we first entered.

"Watch," I tell her. "That's what they want. See his hand moving under the blanket."

She diverts her gaze back to the other couple, her tongue licking over the bottom curve of her mouth.

I want to suck that tongue into my mouth and swallow her groans as they escape from her throat.

Her hand squeezes my thigh, and it takes all of my control not to roll my hips in an effort to entice her to move it up and wrap those delicate, talented fingers around my erection.

As much as I told her I didn't want to be here, I'm not regretting my choice. Seeing the arousal in her eyes, watching the way she shifts in her seat, has a way of turning me on.

I want to play with her, to tease her and make her beg me for more.

"Being here makes me feel naughty," she says, her eyes slow to pull from the working hand of the man a few feet away.

"Me too," I confess. "I want my mouth on every inch of your body, my tongue tasting your skin, your arousal."

She nods, the slightest dip of her chin. "I want that too. Do you think she's wet?"

I cough, an attempt to cover up my surprise. I doubt I'd act that way with any other woman, but I've also never encountered a woman with so little experience. The girl I lost my virginity with even had a few things to educate me on. Lack of experience has never been on my radar before, but knowing she may experience things with me she's never done makes precum leak from the tip of my cock in anticipation.

"I bet she's soaked."

She turns her head in my direction. "That makes two of us."

"Oh yeah?"

She nods again, her eyes dipping to my mouth.

"If you kiss me right now, I might not be able to control myself."

"I thought you didn't want an audience."

"I don't, but I'm really turned on right now."

"Me too," she confesses.

"Maybe we should get up and walk around?"

"That might keep us busy," she agrees, waiting until I stand and offer her my hand before she rises.

She seems a little unsteady on her feet, and fuck if I don't regret coming here. I want nothing more than to lick right up the middle of her and listen to her moans of pleasure.

Thankfully, as we meander around the club, we don't run into a scene where any of the Cerberus guys are performing. I know there are different levels, and some of the more risqué stuff is down the hallways. I make sure to avoid those areas.

I follow her lead, pausing when her feet stutter as she nears a glass wall, a performance with two men and one woman taking place.

I position myself behind her, unable to keep from pulling her against my chest. I press my hand flat against her lower belly, feeling her chest rise and fall as she watches.

"I could never share you like that," I whisper in her ears. "Take in your fill of it tonight, baby, because you'll never experience that."

"It's... I don't know. I always thought that would be painful."

"She looks like she's enjoying it." I turn my attention from her back to the three enjoying each other, not missing the way the man grips the other guy's ass as they seesaw back and forth, one plunging into the woman's pussy while the other pulls from her ass. Back and forth they go, filling and retreating as she moans her pleasure.

"Have you ever done that?"

"Never, but I'd be a willing partner with a toy if it's something you want to try."

She tilts her chin up, looking at me. "Not tonight."

I shake my head. "Not tonight."

Her attention quickly turns back to the performance, her ass pressing against me. I'm so fucking tempted to slide my hand up her dress, but I know someone would see. The couple behind the glass aren't the only ones drawing attention. Just like we watched the man playing with his woman under the blanket, others are touching each other and being watched.

The fact that we're both wearing white bands is enough to police me. If we wanted to do anything else, we'd have to grab a different band. The guy at the counter was adamant about it, and he didn't leave much room for argument. I know the rules are in place to prevent people from being coerced into doing something they don't want to do, and I wouldn't abuse the moment of arousal with Devyn. If she wants more, she'll have to ask for it.

"Watch," I say, my mouth near her throat. "She's going to come."

Devyn reaches down, clasping my hand in hers as the woman moans her release, begging both men to fuck her harder. They comply, making her entire body shake before the man in her ass pulls free and jets cum on her back. The man under her releases inside of her, and then it becomes a battle of who is going to get to lick her clean.

"I love it when those three perform," a woman says to her partner only a few feet from us. "Too bad they never share."

The threesome cuddles together, their hands slow and comforting as they kiss and speak in tones too low for observers to hear.

"Do you think they're like together *together*?" Devyn asks as she leads me away.

I'm glad she steps away from the glass wall because they're no longer performing. It was starting to feel like we were invading an intimate moment, with as much sense as that makes after watching what we just did.

"Possibly. Like Max, Tug, and Jasmine maybe. Those three are all together," I explain.

"I don't think I could do that."

"That dynamic isn't for everyone."

"I'm not complaining, it's just not my thing."

I turn her to face me, ignoring all the others walking around finding something else to watch.

"I could never share you. I don't have any inclination for that kind of lifestyle."

I press my lips to hers, wanting to just give her a quick kiss of reassurance. People are so quick to backpedal when they confess that something isn't for them in fear of offending someone, but there's nothing wrong with knowing something isn't your style.

The kiss doesn't end with a peck. Like the ninja she is, Devyn slips her tongue past my lips, and God help me if it isn't exactly what I wanted.

I hold my hand out, pressing it to the wall to catch our weight as I kiss her back. I get lost in her, lost in the way her body fits against mine as our tongues tangle. I breathe her in, my cock hard and encouraging all sorts of things, but when her hand sweeps down the front of my slacks, I freeze.

I made myself promises about how tonight was going to go, and I'll be damned if I let my arousal talk me out of it. There's nothing wrong with getting freaky in a sex club. And kudos to all the folks that are doing that, but it isn't how I want to spend our first time together. I don't know when I decided on being in this for the long haul with her, but the moment I did I was all in.

"Not yet," I tell her, pulling my face back as I clasp my hand over hers.

I'm not a saint, so I do roll my hips against her touch one last time before pulling her hand away.

"You're so hard."

"You really fucking turn me on," I tell her.

"Same," she says. I somehow find the strength to pull my hand free when she presses my fingers against her inner thigh.

"We have to wait for the other guys," I remind her. "We all rode together."

"You have a rideshare app on your phone, don't you?"

Her eyes sparkle with need as I nod.

"Use it."

27

Devyn

My hands are still trembling, but even as embarrassed as I am about it, Emmett doesn't tease me on the ride back to the hotel.

Instead of using the rideshare app, he texted the other guys to see if they were ready. We waited another half an hour, spending the time at the bar because we were both wound a little too tight to keep watching others enjoy each other, before the guys showed up.

Stormy had a huge smile on his face, his hair a mess as if someone had run their hands through it. Oracle somehow looked more relaxed than he did when he split off from the group. Newton looked bored despite his shirt being buttoned wrong.

They didn't tease me on the drive back. They also didn't go into detail about how they spent their time either, and I was grateful for that.

Wordlessly, Emmett holds his hand out to me as I climb out of the SUV. He doesn't release my hand even when we get on the elevator. I press the button for the sixth floor, trying to stifle a yawn as the car climbs.

"Tired?" he asks, and I shake my head.

I don't want him trying to tuck me into bed and disappearing into his own room.

He lets go of my hand when I reach into my bra to pull out my hotel key card, his eyes staying locked on my chest a little longer than necessary.

The warmth of his body follows me into the hotel room, and I'm grateful. I just knew I was going to have to beg him to join me because he's been so adamant that we need to date and get to know each other before we do anything that we might regret if we discover we aren't compatible.

"I'm going to take a quick shower," I tell him, feeling a little disappointed when he doesn't follow me into the bathroom.

My hands tremble as I undress, scared I'll find my room empty when I'm done.

I take my time, postponing the disappointment. I keep my hair piled on top of my head because I washed it earlier. I pull on a long t-shirt and a pair of panties before going back into the room.

My feet freeze at the sight of him not only still in the room but sitting on the chaise in the corner with a thin blanket on his lap.

"Come here," he insists when it becomes clear that my feet are locked in place.

It takes a minute for my brain to regain control over my body, but he waits patiently, his hand out for me to take as I approach.

I move to straddle him, but he grips my hips and turns me, positioning me between his spread legs before pulling the blanket back up to cover us both.

He doesn't immediately lift my shirt, exposing my breasts like the woman at the club was, but my blood still sings in anticipation of it.

"You liked watching this," he says, his hands situating the blanket perfectly before sliding his own hands under it.

I nod.

"You want to see what it feels like?"

"Emmett," I say, his name on my lips a plea.

"Love my name coming from that pretty mouth, baby. Think you'll be able to say my name with my cock in there?"

I tremble, an involuntary reaction to picturing him taking pleasure from me that way.

Both of his hands skate up my thighs, but he doesn't immediately pull my panties to the side. I know he wants me. The evidence of his own desire is a thick rod at my back, his breath warming my shoulder as he lifts one hand and tugs my sleep shirt off my shoulder.

"I've spent so many hours picturing you in my arms," he says, his tongue tracing the erratic pulse in my throat.

His hands roam, teasing my legs, my side, the very underside of my breasts before disappearing. I feel like a live wire, snapping and pulsing, seeking some kind of validation.

I widen my legs, trying to entice his attention there, but the man refuses to be rushed.

"Emmett," I plead again, my body needy and desperate for more. "Touch me."

He doesn't give me what I want immediately, but I know when he does, it's going to be at the most perfect time. The teasing is part of it, and every brush of his skin against mine is building me up to something spectacular.

Seb didn't make me come. Although he's a couple years older than me, he still seemed inexperienced. No, he seemed selfish. He was quick to force my hand down his pants as he rushed to strip me naked from the bottom down. He went as far as lifting my shirt and pushing my bra over my breasts, but that was for him, not me.

Emmett is pleasing me, and my pleasure pleases him. The difference is so very crystal clear now.

His hands search higher rather than tease lower, pulling a chuckle from his chest when I growl in irritation.

"Shh," he urges. "I'm learning your body."

The growl turns into a whimper when he pinches my nipple over the top of my shirt.

"Can't wait to get my mouth on your perfect tits," he praises, and I sink further against him.

"Same," I pant.

He chuckles. "You seem needy, baby."

"Desperately," I confess.

"Yeah?" His voice is soft, but that doesn't stop the rumble of pleasure from his chest when I lift my arm and expose my left breast to the cool air.

"So fucking naughty." His hand travels lower, the tips of his fingers teasing the side of my panties. "Is this what you wanted?"

I hate the disconnect with being able to feel his touch but only being able to see his hand move under the blanket. I pull the blanket off, spreading my legs wider as I do.

"Need to watch," I say on a hiss when he traces my slit over my panties, the silk embarrassingly wet and damn near transparent.

I feel him shift, moving his body so he can watch over my shoulder.

"Jesus, Devyn."

"I know," I manage on a moan as he pulls the ruined silk to the side, revealing my most intimate parts.

"You have the prettiest pussy," he praises, his fingers dipping into my arousal.

The sensation is so shocking, I try to clamp my legs closed.

"We can't have that, now can we?" he says, lifting his own legs and locking them over the top of mine as he forces them to spread all the way open.

I feel exposed and a little powerless. Somehow it turns me on instead of making me want to ask him to stop.

"Goddamn," he hisses when he dips his finger into my opening. "Gonna come the second I try to wedge my cock into this tight pussy."

I whimper again, my hips trying to move as he presses his pointer finger all the way inside. I've never experienced pleasure like this. My body feels like it's being hit over and over by lightning.

My moan matches his groan when my body reflexively clenches around the intrusion. His other hand grips my breast, his fingers toying with the tightened nipple, and it's just too much. He's a hundred percent focused on my body, but I'm incapable of controlling any of my reactions. They're being determined by his attention.

I notice the tremble in my muscles first, little spasms that quickly turn into jolts and convulsions along my arms and legs.

"Give into it," he commands. "Let that sweet little pussy come."

I don't know why my instinct is to force his hand away. I've orgasmed before while touching myself, but what's happening now isn't on the same level.

I know what he's doing is going to leave me drained and completely pleased, so there's no sense in fighting it. I'm no longer in control.

"That's it," he praises when my back arches and I chase his hand with the swirl of my hips.

There are so many things going on—his breath on my shoulder and neck, the beat of his own racing heart at my back, his thick erection against my ass.

"Emmett," I whimper.

"I've got you, baby. Let go."

I swear my eyes roll back and for a few glorious moments, I'm floating, the two fingers he has in me the only thing anchoring me.

He praises me through the orgasm, his voice husky and full of awe. I never knew the words good girl were such a damn turn-on for me, but his use of them prolongs my orgasm, taking it to a higher level.

I feel depleted when it ends, my breath catching in my throat in a way that makes it sound like I have hiccups.

His hand is resting against my clit, the warmth of his palm absorbing the electric zings as they periodically spark. His other hand is resting on my hip, his fingers curled into my flesh as if he thinks I may try to run away.

He stops me when I try to turn around, but before I can get upset, he makes his intentions clear. He pulls a condom from the other and presents it to me.

I reach for it with trembling fingers because I'm still suffering the effects of the full-body orgasm.

"Just hold," he says. "Need to get my cock out."

With one strong hand, he lifts me, giving him room with his other hand to unzip his slacks. When he lowers me back down, I can focus on nothing but the fiery heat of his manhood at my ass. It has to be ten degrees warmer than the rest of him.

He adjusts himself, sliding down some in the chair and lifting me so I'm sitting on his lower belly, his thick, jutting erection between my legs.

I look down at it because there's no way to fight the need to see it, and I have to swallow. He used the word wedge earlier when goading me about sex, and the man will have to do just that. He's thick and dark, the skin pulled tight, the veins pulsing along the sides. I haven't seen many dicks. Seb was so quick to get started there was no amount of foreplay before he had the condom on and was pushing inside of me.

"Jesus," he groans when I run the tip of one finger down the side of it. "Condom?"

I place the package in his hand when he asks for it, watching in awe as he opens the package and rolls the thing down without even having to see since I'm blocking his view.

"That seems rote," I complain.

"Now is not the time to remind me that I'm fucking thirty, Devyn. I've had a dick for a long time."

I huff a laugh, but it quickly turns into a whimper of need when he wraps his full fist around his condom-covered dick.

He uses his other hand to tease me, his fingers sliding through my desire but never really pressing where I need him to.

I want to beg, but I don't have the courage. I'm not even facing him and just thinking of asking for what I want makes my cheeks flame. What if I say it wrong? What if I sound stupid? What if we get started and he doesn't enjoy it?

This was so much easier when he was controlling the situation, but it seems he's giving me a choice. I know what I want, I just don't know how to ask for it or take it.

With a lighter grip on himself, he slaps the tip against my slit, sending another zing of awareness and need through my body.

"Lift up," he says, his hand cupped under my ass for assistance.

I do the best I can, but my legs are splayed out, still trapped by his. He does most of the work in lifting me, directing my body down until his dick is wedged at my entrance.

I'm soaked, the orgasm he drew from me assisting in coating me in slickness, but I know it's still going to be a tight fit. The press of the second finger earlier felt almost too much.

"Emmett?"

He freezes, the darkened head of his cock kissing the lips of my pussy.

"Want to stop?"

I shake my head, uncertain of how to express the fear bubbling inside of me.

I'm not a virgin. I made that declaration to him before, but he doesn't even compare to Seb.

"Scared," I manage, the word weak.

"Want me to stop?" There's no accusation or disappointment in his voice.

If I tell him yes, I know he'll pull away. I also know he isn't going to hold it against me or treat me differently.

I think that's what gives me the courage I need.

"Maybe just go slow. I don't think it will fit."

He huffs a laugh. "God, baby, you're good for my ego."

I shake my head as he presses against me once again. "It wasn't a compliment. You're too big."

"Jesus, Devyn. Do you want me to come in three seconds?"

He presses against me again, the heat of him right where I didn't know I needed to be warmed.

"That's it, baby. Slowly."

I bite my lip as I begin to sink down on him, my body accepting him when I thought it couldn't. The stretch and pull is almost addictive, that little zing of pain somehow just as needed as the fullness pressing into me.

"God. Damn," he grunts through his teeth, his fingers a bruising grip on my hip. "Nope."

In the next breath, he pulls me off, standing from the chair as if I weigh nothing.

I expect him to press me face down into the bed, but he turns me around on my back, and I watch in awe as he starts pulling at his clothes.

28

LEGACY

How fucked up is it that I hope she translates the way I abruptly pulled her off of me as just wanting to get undressed or that I want to be face-to-face when we do this rather than the truth, which is I couldn't even get her fully seated on my cock before the threat of orgasm started inching up my spine?

I've built this up in my head, fantasized about it, shamefully closed my eyes in the shower after accepting how badly I wanted her. Those conjured imaginings have nothing on the way her body gripped mine those few seconds.

My erection juts forward proudly from my opened slacks as if pointing to its one and only desire as I unbutton my shirt. I'm going slow, needing every damn second to get my shit together. But with the way she's watching my fingers work open each button, she doesn't seem inconvenienced by it. I carelessly toss my shirt to the side, watching her face as I once again wrap my hand around my cock in a punishing grip.

My list of desires is easily a mile long, possibly two, but my first time with this beautiful woman won't be spent checking things off one by one. I just need to be inside of her. My body is desperate for it.

I want to instruct her to touch herself, to slide her dainty fingers through the slickness there, but watching her do it wouldn't help the threat of premature orgasm I'm still fighting.

"Do you have any idea how fucking sexy you are?"

"You make me feel like I'm the only woman you see," she whispers, her fingers gripping the comforter at her hips.

"Pull your shirt off."

She obeys without question, her perky tits tipped with tightened nipples.

I kick my slacks away, needing to clench my hand in order to keep from stroking my aching cock.

"The panties too."

In seconds, she's naked, every inch of her body exposed to me. I see the tremble in her hands. I know she's nervous, but I bet her need will win out over everything else.

"Spread your legs," I say, her quickness to obey making the last word end on a moan as she does as I ask. "Fuck, baby."

I take a step forward, loving the way her arms lift, reaching for me.

It's all too damn intense.

"I want you to know we can stop at any time." She shakes her head, rejecting my offer.

"This is what I want."

"I want it too," I say, but feel the need to clarify. "But this isn't all I want from you, Devyn. Sex is a benefit to what we're building, but it isn't everything. I need you to understand that."

A slow smile tugs at her cheeks. "So you'll want to cuddle after?"

"It makes you mine," I clarify.

"You already claimed me," she says, her breath wispy and full of need. "Now you can take me."

I continue to fight the urge to just shove inside of her, having more control over my body than I originally thought, as I crawl up her body on the bed, pressing my lips to the thrum of her pulse in her neck.

Her hands are warm on my exposed skin, her fingers curling into my back when I pull back a few inches.

Her lips beckon me, and I'm done resisting the temptation that is her. I don't think I could walk away even under the threat of death. Although I don't understand the connection, I'm no longer strong enough to fight it.

"Mine," I whisper against her cheek before pressing my lips to hers.

I lick into her mouth, my tongue swiping at hers until I have to take a breath. My lips make a trail down her body, her skin covered in goosebumps. I love how reactive her body is to my touch, her nipples beading when I suck one into my mouth. Her back arches, her mouth opening, a nearly silent cry falling from her lips.

I make my way lower, licking and tasting her skin, but knowing it'll never be enough. I aim to spend an eternity with my mouth on her skin.

The scent of her arousal slams into me as I tease her belly button with the tip of my tongue. I turn into a feral animal, one that probably couldn't be held back if someone tried.

"Emmett!" she screeches at the first swipe of my tongue against her clit.

I moan at the way she grips my hair in her ineffectual fingers. The sting in my scalp is only part of the arousing puzzle we're working on together.

With my arms under her legs, my hands cupped over, I hold her in place, desperate to know what it feels like for her to come on my tongue. She doesn't disappoint, her body giving me exactly what I need in mere seconds.

I need this to last, but my insistent body is working on a compromise I can't help but agree with. Hard and fast now, just to take the edge off, and then slow and exploratory later.

My lips are glistening with her orgasm, but that doesn't stop her from pulling me up, her mouth angled toward mine as I settle between her legs.

The kiss is fiery and full of need, the orgasm she just had only half of what her body is demanding from me. I pull my hips back, a hundred percent ready to oblige whatever she demands of me.

I keep my eyes locked on her face. The pinch of pain she'll feel is unavoidable. I know she isn't a virgin, but it's clear she hasn't done much. Every touch seems like a new experience, and I hate that asshole she mentioned before even more. She deserves to be cherished, worshipped, given everything she could imagine and then some.

"Feel me," I say when I press forward, my cock demanding that I shove fully inside of her.

She nods, her head jerking as if she's losing some motor function.

"I'm yours," I tell her. "Take me."

Her mouth hangs open, her eyes wide as I press in further. Her fingers are curled into my flesh but she's trying to tug me closer, not attempting to push me away.

When she spreads her legs wider, wrapping her ankles around my thighs, I nearly lose my fucking mind.

"Good girl," I praise, her eyes lighting up. I have to smile at finding another thing she likes so much.

My cock jerks, the threat of orgasm right on the surface that quickly.

"Feel good?" I ask, my own eyes rolling back when she flexes those inner muscles as if trying to determine her answer.

"Yes," she pants. "For you?"

"The best fucking thing I've ever felt in my life, Devyn. You're addictive. Don't know how we'll ever be able to get anything done."

She chuckles, a movement that makes her body grip me even tighter.

I pull back, slowly pressing forward again, and her mouth hangs open even further.

I set a pace that I feel like I can maintain, watching her with every push forward and retreat. The muscles in my back threaten to lock up, my balls drawing tight against my body.

When she leans forward, coming up to rest on her elbows so she can watch my intrusion, I nearly lose it again. I press my forehead to hers, both of us locking our eyes on our connection.

"See how well you take me?"

I feel her head dip in acknowledgment, her breath growing more and more ragged, telling me she not only enjoys what's happening but my words turn her on as well.

"Touch your clit."

Her hands are shaking as she reaches it, but she perseveres, her small hand working that delicious knot of nerves quickly. God, I would drain my bank account to pay for a front-row seat of watching her do just that for an hour.

"Baby," I pant. "You're making me come."

For a flash of a second, I want to rip the condom off and fill her up with my cum. I want everything that could possibly accompany that action. The baby. The tits full of milk.

I'm breathless as my cock kicks inside of her, my mind racing as I consider the possibility of a newfound fucking kink because the idea of breeding her, putting my baby inside of her, slams into me like a ten-ton truck.

The pulse of my orgasm is unlike any other I've experienced in my lifetime.

"Emmett," she moans, her hand working faster and faster, and then she falls, the clamp of her around me prolonging my own orgasm until I'm scared I'll crush her.

I fall to the side mere inches from on top of her.

The tremble in her muscles matches mine as we both remain silent, basking in the afterglow.

There's no urge to pull away, no warning bells going off in my head that this was a mistake.

As much as I claimed this woman, I let my eyes flutter closed, knowing full well she fucking owns me.

29

Devyn

Unlike the night I spent with Seb, Emmett never pulled away from me.

He held me in his arms until we were both capable of functioning again before guiding me to the bathroom for a shower. I got three hours of sleep before he woke me, once again with his head between my legs. I had no idea sex could be like this. I didn't have a clue that my pleasure would ever be something that gave a man his own pleasure. He wants me to orgasm. He demanded it of my body, which was so willing to obey him.

When we were exhausted and ready to sleep, he pulled me to him, skin to skin, and held me in his arms all night.

When we woke again with the sun peeping through the curtains, he demanded more from me, and of course I willingly gave all he needed.

I should be walking on clouds, and in my mind I was until we joined the three other guys in the lobby. He stayed close, was quick to wrap his arm around my back, but he also volunteered to drive, which put the console of the SUV between us. He could've easily allowed one of the other guys to drive and I could be in his arms, snuggled against his chest. I feel like I've lost something, and I don't know exactly how to deal with it.

Maybe he regrets what happened, or he feels shame. He didn't hesitate to help me into the passenger seat, but he's studiously watching the road. I haven't caught him glancing my way once since the drive started.

Maybe it's my immaturity. Maybe I'm pulling my expectations from the wrong group of people, but the boys in high school were all over their girlfriends between classes and during gym. They'd risk getting into trouble just to kiss their lips or grab a handful of their asses.

He claimed me, but only in private. Other than the arm around me, he has made no declarations to the other guys.

I clench my jaw, hating that my head is even taking me in this direction. He's not a boy. He's a grown man, and he doesn't have to growl and snap at other people to assert his ownership. But that doesn't stop that neglected part inside of me that needs that in some form from him. I've been in the shadows, a second thought for far too long. The abandoned little girl who is still cowering in the corner, needing to be noticed, expected more from him.

As we cover the miles back to Farmington, my mood sours. By the time we pull into the parking lot at Cerberus, I'm livid, eight hours of scenarios deep in my head.

I climb out of the SUV before Emmett can make his way around to open the door from me. Oracle offers me my overnight bag, and I give him a halfhearted thanks before walking away.

A low growl rumbles from my throat when a hand clasps mine, but I don't argue. Losing my shit in front of an audience really isn't my style.

Emmett guides me into the clubhouse, the other members growing silent when we enter. I feel like I'm on display, but the joy I thought I'd feel with his ownership is absent as everyone watches us.

We have to walk in front of the television to get to the hallway that leads to the newer section of the clubhouse, but no one complains. I doubt they're paying much attention to the horse race that's playing on it anyway.

"Atta boy," Stormy says at our back just as he heads down the hallway toward Emmett's room.

I don't have very long to look around his room before he's standing right in front of me, his hand on my cheek.

He leans forward, his lips brushing mine. I wish I could say that I pulled away, but I'm not strong enough to resist him, and I'm easily lost in the kiss.

An alarm sounds in my head, a warning that getting lost in him and ignoring red flags will only lead to me getting hurt.

I pull back, swallowing roughly at the site of his slick, kissable lips.

"You ignore me for eight hours and now you want to kiss me?"

I take a step back from him, but his arm around my waist tightens, preventing me from going far.

"I've wanted my lips on yours every second since I woke up," he says.

I shake my head, feeling like he's trying to manipulate me.

"Hey." He presses closer.

"It's nothing." I try to wave him off, the threat of tears burning the backs of my eyes, but he doesn't allow the reprieve.

"It's not nothing. Talk to me."

"Are we a secret? Do you want to fuck me, but I'm not good enough to—"

The rage in his eyes makes me want to cower, but there's a part of me deep inside that assures me this man would never hurt me. I don't know if listening to that voice is a mistake.

"I didn't know how you wanted me to act. I didn't know if you'd be embarrassed if I kissed you or touched you in front of the guys."

I open my mouth but no sound comes out.

"Clearly I made the wrong move, but never doubt that I want you or that you're mine. I'll claim you in front of the entire club."

"You're not embarrassed to be with me?"

"Embarrassed?" He shakes his head. "I'm the luckiest fucker around, Devyn. I want everyone to know you're mine."

I clear my throat. Apologies have never been easy for me. It's always been hard for me to accept that I've made a mistake because it gives the other person, namely my parents, more reason to reject me.

"I let my emotions get the best of me," I confess. "I'm sorry. I don't want to be one of those people who just lets things fester when we could solve the issue with a conversation."

His thumb gently swipes over my face, his eyes locked on my lips. "I don't want that either."

"I'm sorry," I say again.

"Want me to take you out there and plant a kiss on your lips in front of everyone? Or do you want me to strip you naked and eat your pussy until you scream? Either way would let them know you're mine."

I blink up at him.

"Is that moving too fast?" he challenges.

I scoff. "I may be what you consider mature for my age, but don't say stuff like that. The girl in me wants to swoon, and I'm sure I'd marry you tomorrow if you asked, and—"

I clamp my mouth closed, my hands coming up to cover my lips for good measure.

His grin is wide.

"I'm sorry. God, I didn't mean that, I mean, maybe I did, but—shit."

He chuckles, his hand reaching up and pulling my hand from my face.

"This," he says, running his fingers over my heated cheeks. "This is so damn sexy to me."

"My embarrassment?"

He nods. "The way your emotions play out on your skin. This pink is the same as when you come. It's intoxicating. I want to see it all the time. But as much as I love the color, I don't want you to ever be embarrassed around me. We can have hard conversations. You can tell me what you're feeling. I don't want you to worry that it'll make me walk away from you. I'm not going anywhere."

I let him lead me into his en suite, not arguing when he starts to strip me naked. My body is humming with anticipation, fully aware of his talents and eagerness to make my body sing for him.

"As long as we're being mature," he begins, lifting my hands and guiding my fingers to the clasp and zipper of his jeans.

I start to strip him as well, the coolness in the room licking at my overheated skin but incapable of cooling me down.

"I want you to know that I don't think Vaughn would be okay with what's happening between us."

My hands freeze on the waistband of his jeans.

"I say that because he had a huge problem with one of our friends in high school who got caught sneaking around with another friend's sister."

I do not want to talk about nor think about my deceased brother right now, but Emmett is right. We need to be able to have these conversations.

"Maybe he had more of a problem with the immaturity of the sneaking around than the guy coming forward and telling the friend what his intentions were?" I challenge.

"Asking?" he says, but I shake my head.

"Permission is ridiculous. A sibling doesn't have any right to dictate who a brother or sister can date. I'm not just saying that because of our situation and the stance you think Vaughn would take. What if they were soulmates, and the guy got in the way of that? It isn't fair to anyone involved."

"I think the guy didn't want his sister getting hurt."

"That's not his call either. People need to be able to live their own lives, and mistakes in life are how we learn."

"You're eighteen," he says, grabbing my hand before I can slip it down the front of his jeans.

"And you're thirty, still in your prime."

"Being with me means you will experience life less. I think Vaughn would have an opinion on that."

"People experience life in order to make choices. There's no harm in making the right choice right from the start."

He swallows when I look up at him, his concern drawing his eyebrows together.

"You're afraid I'll end up thinking this was the wrong choice?"

His silence is his answer.

"I can't predict the future, Emmett, but I don't think I'm ever going to look back and think that I could've been happier without you. I think I'm here because this is exactly where I was supposed to be, but if you have doubts."

He clings to my hands, preventing me from walking away.

"I know you're it for me, Devyn. I know it because I have experienced life. My choice comes because of the things I've experienced."

"Not everyone has to make a hundred mistakes before getting it right," I challenge with a smirk.

"There has not been a hundred... mistakes," he says.

"Does this conversation change your mind about us?"

He shakes his head. "Not a chance, but I'm willing to—"

"Let me make my own choice then. I know what I want."

"You'll tell me if you change your mind?"

"I won't change my mind, but yes. If you need to hear that I'll tell you if I decide I'm no longer interested in you, will keep you from stopping my hand in your pants, then yes. I will tell if something changes."

"Promise?"

"I swear to you. Now will you teach me how to suck your cock? I've never done it before."

His eyes light on fire, his hand not wasting a second before tangling in my hair as I lower to my knees, taking his jeans down his thighs with me.

30

LEGACY

"You don't find that gross?" she asks, her cheeks flushed with my new favorite shade of pink.

I lick into her mouth, my cum coating her tongue making me groan with renewed arousal.

"Did you find it gross when I kissed you after eating your pussy?"

She shakes her head. "It was hot."

"Same goes for me."

The girl just sucked my soul from my cock, her eagerness to learn more of a turn-on than anything else.

"We're going to run out of hot water," she says, taking a step back.

She's naked, having no argument on her lips when I stripped her bare.

The water of the shower cascades over her, dampening her hair. She's a fucking goddess, everything in life I didn't know I had a right to ask for.

I think she's way off the mark about Vaughn. I don't think asking him to date her would get me anywhere other than a bloody nose. I think the same would go for her parents, although the age gap wouldn't be so much an issue as them swearing I'm the reason they lost their son.

I should probably pause, take a beat to consider everyone else involved, but what she said before hitting her knees resonates with me.

What if they were soulmates?

I feel that far down into my chest as humanly possible. I know it's too soon to even think these things, but I don't feel as if I'm in control any longer. There's another force at work, something guiding me to her, something making me rethink the words I said earlier about Vaughn not approving.

I feel like I'm losing my mind a little. I'm not one to believe in fate or the afterlife, or ghosts on any level. I'm as far from a religious man as one could probably get, but arguing about a vengeful God that lets horrific things happen to innocent people has no place in this shower with us right now. Needless to say, my beliefs in such things are non-existent.

It still doesn't stop that urgency deep inside of me to wrap my arms around her and never let go. Claiming her, declaring her mine has less to do with sexual reference and everything to do with stepping up and being the man who will protect her for the rest of my life.

I stare down at her, sacred words a breath away from escaping my lips.

I choke them down, her own declarations not enough for me to trust that she wouldn't feel overwhelmed by them.

I cup my hand to her cheek, her eyes blinking up at me, so bright and full of the millions of things she hasn't encountered yet. I want to be there by her side when she learns new things, when she sees new places, when she discovers the things in life she loves and hates. I want to hold her hand through the things that scare her and stand by her side when she discovers her own strengths. I want to be the man she leans on when she can't muster the courage to face something alone.

"I—" I begin, but the words clog my throat, the warning that it's much too soon, that saying them opens me up for pain.

Losing her brother was the hardest thing I've faced in life. It gutted me. It changed me. It made me cautious of ever putting myself in a situation where I'd risk it happening again, but denying my feelings for her don't diminish them. Avoiding any pain that may come is already too late.

"Emmett," she says, taking a step closer to me. "What's wrong?"

There's still a part inside of me that remembers the shattered dreams, how much Vaughn's death altered my path in life. I also know it has nothing on what losing her would do to me, and there's a level of guilt that comes with that. Vaughn and I were inseparable. We spent every day together for years, and somehow this woman has managed to surpass that connection in a matter of weeks. It should feel like a betrayal, and I can't decide if that pressure at my back pushing me toward her is something ethereal or my own creation in trying to convince myself that loving her is okay.

"I want you to come to Texas with me," I say, unsure of how what I was going to say would be received.

"Texas?"

I nod, swallowing the threat of emotions I don't understand myself.

"Jinx's brother is getting married. They had some bad stuff happen in their town, and they'd feel more comfortable if some of us guys were in attendance."

"Is it dangerous?"

I lean into the press of her hand on my chest.

"No. It's a small sleepy little town, that just somehow ended up on the wrong group's radar. I wouldn't invite you if I thought you were in danger."

I say this with confidence because there's confirmation that Raul Cortez has been killed, his entire organization broken up and dismantled.

"I have a lot of orders."

I tilt her chin up. "I love how dedicated you are to your work, but you need breaks too, remember?"

She nods. "When is it?"

"Two weeks from yesterday," I answer. "I've seen your schedule. I think you can manage a long weekend so long as you don't take more orders."

"I'm not going to turn down orders," she argues, the stubborn streak making me want to kiss her until it's gone, but then I know I'll miss the fire in her eyes.

"Let them know you have that weekend off."

I step in closer to her, pressing my renewed erection against her lower belly.

"You're not fighting fair," she says, her mouth hanging open when I bend my knees and roll my hips against her center.

"I know."

"I'll go with you on one condition," she barters. "Do that thing you did last night."

"What thing?"

Her cheeks flame once again.

"That thing you did with your tongue and fingers."

I swear I could come on her wet skin.

That thing being sucking her clit into my mouth while teasing both her pussy and her ass at the same time.

"My pleasure," I say, loving the way she squeals with excitement when I pick her up and carry her out of the bathroom.

She didn't exactly choose option two, the one where I make her scream so the others in the clubhouse know she's mine, but that's exactly what she ended up with.

31

Devyn

"If you keep wiggling like that..." There's a hint of warning in his tone, but the punishment he's hinting at is something I can't ever get enough of, so the threat falls flat.

"I'm cold," I complain, sweeping my hand up his thigh and barely brushing the side of his morning erection.

"You're a damn furnace. How are you cold?"

I snuggle deeper, loving the rumble of his chest and the way he presses his palm to my back, pulling me closer.

Unable to resist, I lift my leg and throw it over the top of his, grinding myself against his thigh. He doesn't say a word, but his hand on my back moves lower, a single finger tracing my ass cheek.

I'm certain this man could do anything he pleases to my body, and I'd only ask for more after I caught my breath.

It's been two weeks of us making love, two weeks of waking up in his arms because he warned me the first night that if I stayed in his bed, he'd never let me leave.

I don't know if he knew it or not, but I needed that reassurance. I needed him to tell me he wanted me there because I would've felt awkward if he hadn't. I would've gotten lost in my head wondering if I was wearing out my welcome. He either needs me beside him just as much or he's an expert at reading me and knowing exactly what I need.

There have been no hiccups, not one moment where I look over at him and think he's not happy. He's always smiling, always wanting to touch me in some way, even if it's to simply pull me to his side.

Despite him marching me through the clubhouse after our trip to Denver, he hasn't faltered in showing me attention in front of the other Cerberus members. He didn't shy away when Kincaid came into the living room and I was sitting on his lap. Kincaid simply smiled at the two of us, wrapped his arm around his smiling wife, and continued the conversation he was having with Shadow. It was proof of his approval. I didn't know how much I needed that from Em either. She's been more like a mother to me than I can ever recall my own being, but she's like that with a lot of us here.

After speaking with several of the others, the lost and looking for a family seems to be a theme. Khloe had no one decades ago when Kid found her. Even Em had to have Kincaid step in when she was being abused by her ex-husband.

Cerberus has provided a loving and nurturing family, and they ask nothing in return other than being respectful and caring to the next person who needs their help. There are no ulterior motives here. These people aren't building trust just so they can manipulate people. I feel like I found the tribe I've always been meant to find.

It eases the ache of not being wanted by my parents, even though Emmett insists that they're just hurting and they don't know how to channel that pain. It doesn't explain why Quincy doesn't answer the phone when I call and only responds with short answers when I text. All of it would be too much to handle if it weren't for the people here who welcomed me with open arms.

"I don't think we have time for that," Emmett grumbles as I roll my hips once again.

"I already packed," I argue, thinking there are always a few minutes we can steal from the day.

I learned that a lot can be accomplished in a fifteen-minute break if we just put our minds to it.

"What are you wearing to the wedding?"

"You remember that silk dressing gown I found the other day?"

He rumbles his acknowledgment, but I can hear the displeasure in the sound.

Smiling against his chest, I continue, "I added sequins and beads to the top and made the fit a little better for my frame."

"That thing barely went past your ass."

"It's a little sexy," I confirm. "I think I'll pair it with those red heels I was able to repair."

I keep my mouth against him, each word brushing my lips against his chest. His arm around me tightens, his pulse kicking up a notch.

"You don't like the dress?"

"The dress is sexy as hell, but maybe it's a bad idea to wear it."

"To a wedding?"

"In public," he clarifies.

I pull my head back, my eyes narrowing. "I never took you for a man who would get growly and tell me I can't wear something."

His smile is slow and a little sinister. "Make no mistake, baby. I'm not saying you can't wear it, but know if you do, there will be consequences."

I push further away, my hands pressed to his chest so I can look down at him fully.

"Consequences?"

"Not for you, but I'll throat punch every guy that eyeballs you. It may ruin the day."

I chew the inside of my cheek in a failed attempt to keep from smiling.

"Are you fucking with me?" he growls, my lip twitching with the need to laugh.

"Have I told you how hot your jealousy is?"

He dips his head. "Just last week, remember?"

I take a fortifying breath, ready to repeat the same argument we had then. "Oracle isn't competition. He says that shit to get a rise out of you and you let him every single time."

His jaw flexes, no doubt remembering the altercation.

"He asked you to bend over again because he missed it the first time."

"I was wearing sweats."

"Do you have any idea how great your ass looks in sweats?"

I huff a humorless laugh. "No ones ass looks good in sweats."

I nip at his chin playfully.

Without warning, he pulls me on top of him, and I have no choice but to straddle his naked body.

"It's too early in the day for this, Devyn."

I roll my hips, loving the way his eyes drop to the space between my legs. The man is just as obsessed with me as I am with him.

"I still haven't decided whether or not I'm going to punch Oracle in the face."

"I'm yours," I remind him on a low moan when he presses his thumb to my clit.

"Prove it," he grumbles.

I press my legs deeper into the mattress and lift myself up enough to notch his dick against my entrance.

"You're playing with fire, Devyn."

I know he'd have no issue with me taking him inside of me bare. He's not the type of guy who would shirk his responsibilities if we were to create a life. But in our maturity and while we were fully clothed, making it easier to discuss, we decided babies now would be too soon although we had agreed it was something we both wanted.

I lift off, letting his dick slap against his stomach. I know it's something I'll have to work through but there's still that voice in my head that tells me I need to do everything to make sure he stays. If I had his baby, he'd never leave. He's the type of man who will always take care of his responsibilities. It's crazy, bordering on psychotic, to want to trap him, and that's what it would boil down to. I don't want to be that person, but past trauma tries to convince me that something other than me is necessary to keep him, as if I can't accept that I'm enough for him.

"Just another week or so," he says, reminding me of the birth control I recently started. "Believe me, I can't wait to see my cum dripping from you."

I nod, knowing he's right. I have so many goals to reach in life before having kids.

"But in the meantime," he says, sliding down the bed while simultaneously pulling me further up his body.

All cognizant thought is lost with the first swipe of his heated tongue.

"I love that look in your eyes," he whispers.

I'm incapable of pulling my eyes from the window.

"I've never been to Texas," I say.

"There's more to Texas than this airport. I want to show you the world, baby."

I cover his hand on my thigh with my own, turning my head to look at him.

"I don't need the world," I say with a swallow.

He leans closer, pressing his lips to mine before I can get all emotional again.

I'm in that weird place of being ecstatically happy but also cautious that I've been given too many great things and karma has to step in to even it all out.

His lips are soft and warm on mine, gentle and kind, and full of all the things we just haven't said to each other yet.

I've been following his lead, matching his confessions one for one because I don't want to scare him. I don't want to put myself out there entirely only for him to start pulling back because it's just too much for him to handle. He was so adamant in the beginning that we couldn't happen, it makes me cautious that he'll go back to that train of thought.

His hand cups my cheek when he pulls his mouth away.

"You missed your chance to initiate me into the mile high club," I say, knowing that kiss turned him on as much as it did me.

I pray we never lose that fire, that every kiss will always have the potential to lead to more.

"And I told you before you snuck off to the bathroom that you're a screamer, and you'd never survive the embarrassment."

My cheeks heat with the reminder. That day after Denver when he took me to his room for the first time, things got loud in his room. When we came out, heading to the kitchen for something to eat a couple hours later, we entered the living room to a round of applause. I could've died of humiliation.

"After you," Stormy says with humor in his tone.

I look over to see him standing near the open door of the plane, waiting for us to rise from our seats.

Emmett rises, muttering something about cockblocking despite his insistence that it couldn't happen.

His hand is warm against mine as I stand, but before I can walk toward the door, he stops me and lifts my chin so I'm looking him in the eye.

"I will take you any place you ever want to go. We'll get many more chances to join that club." He presses a quick kiss to my lips. "I'm not a member either, but maybe I'll charter a private jet and make sure the door to the cockpit is closed."

I lick his taste from my lips and nod my agreement.

"I can't wait," I whisper.

32

LEGACY

"I never knew places like this existed," Devyn says, awe in her voice as we walk down the street in Lindell.

"Not many do."

The town is quaint and as close-knit as a community can get. It's one of those places where everyone knows everyone else, and there are never any secrets because there's always someone sticking their nose in someone else's business, but not in an insanely annoying way. The people here don't have a problem with asking questions even when the information may be private. The clubhouse isn't much different. Everyone there is in everyone's business as well.

"Jinx is from here?"

"Yeah. He has a brother and sister, and his parents are here as well. Well, his mom and stepdad."

"I haven't seen a Dollar Store."

I chuckle. Dollar Stores have spread like wildfire everywhere.

"I think they have town rules about corporate businesses. They only want private owned, less commercial businesses in town," I explain, wondering how defensive everyone got when the hotel was built out on the highway which technically is only a few yards outside of the city limits.

"That's adorable," she says, pointing to the pet store across the street. "Endless Pawsibilities, and the vet's office? Raise the Woof? That's so creative."

I figured the artist and designer in her would appreciate this place more than the average person would.

"How was the luncheon?"

"Everyone was so nice. I thought I'd feel out of place, but they were so welcoming, if a little nosy. I think one of the cousins from out of town has her sights set on Stormy though." She chuckles as her eyes continue to wander. "She asked so many questions."

"He can handle his own," I assure her.

I'm trying to figure out a way to bring up the conversation I had earlier with Jinx, but I don't want to hurt her feelings. We have this thing about facing the hard conversations and not letting them fester so they don't cause problems, but I also know the age thing has been an issue in the past.

"Want to tell me why you're twitchy?"

I shake my head. The woman has an uncanny ability to read me like an open book.

"After the meet and greet," I begin.

"Ah!" she snaps. "I forgot to tell you. McKenna invited me to a little girls' night thing. I told her I'd check with you."

"Jinx invited me to a little guys' night thing at The Hairy Frog."

Her cute little nose scrunches. "The Hairy—"

"It's the local bar. I think it's going to be like a bachelor type thing."

She chews the inside of her cheek the way she does when she's planning to act differently than she feels. I love it when she does that, so I keep my mouth shut and let it happen.

"You're leaving me tonight for strippers?"

I tilt my head. "It's a college town. They're just working their way through school."

She huffs a laugh, her cheeks pulling up with her smile as she swipes a hand out and smacks my arm playfully. "You're rotten!"

I pull her to my chest. "I don't think there will be strippers. You'd be welcome to come along if you wanted, but there's a twenty-one and up rule unless you're there with a parent." I press my lips to hers when she opens her mouth to speak. "No fucking 'be my daddy' jokes either."

Her laughter is contagious. "If you can predict everything I'm going to say, I think you'll grow bored with me quickly."

"Never," I vow. "If you don't want me to go, I'll stay with you."

"You can't stay with me. I'm going to the girls' night thing, and no guys are allowed."

She takes a step back and pats my chest, and it gets my hackles up.

"Will there be strippers?"

She shrugs, her eyes sparkling with mischief.

"If there are, it's a college town. They're simply working their way through college."

"Nearly every person here is on some type of scholarship. Lindell University is known for churning out athletes. You may not know this but Kid's son and Colton's son are graduates from here."

I won't go into more detail about recent trouble and the run-in with one of Angel Guerra's men. She sees a sleepy little town that has somehow kept up with certain aspects of modern living, but has also managed to hold on to some pretty important old-school morals that many other places haven't.

I know that a college student and a guardian were abducted from the school parking lot last year and forced into sex trafficking. I know that, although they weren't hurt, Landon, Rick, and two other students were held captive by a psycho who was supposed to keep an eye on the female, but he deemed it too much work and took all four of them captive instead. I also know that Cerberus is here as a warning to anyone who might want to cause problems.

We don't expect problems, but there's always a possibility.

"On a different note," she says, that same sparkle in her eyes. "Do you have a hundred dollars I can borrow, preferably in ones?"

She squeals in delight, drawing the attention of several people walking down the sidewalk when I lift her up and tickle her at the same time. I put her down almost immediately because I see fear in one woman's eyes. She hasn't decided if I'm a friend or a foe, but she legit looks like she's getting ready to take a chance and pull a damn gun from her purse in order to defend Devyn.

I lift my hand to let her know I'm not a bad man and pull Devyn into my side. The woman seems satisfied when Devyn reaches up on her toes and presses a kiss to my cheek.

"I was joking," she whispers. "Ones are outdated. I'll need fives."

"Everyone in this place is happy and you look like you're being forced to chew glass." Jinx knocks his beer bottle against mine, forcing me to move quickly to prevent it from falling over.

"Do you know what the women had planned tonight?" I ask.

Jinx shakes his head. "Painting their toenails and gossiping about us?"

"Devyn mentioned strippers."

Jinx chuckled. "No way. Reagan would've told me."

He takes another sip of his beer, but suddenly he's no longer looking like he's having a good time.

"You two look like someone took your toy and taunted you with it before running away."

I attempt to smile at Kalen, Jinx's younger brother and the man getting married tomorrow, but it feels awkward on my face.

"So," Jinx says, his attempt at nonchalance sounding anything but. "What were the girls doing tonight?"

"Collins managed to round up a couple guys from the school to—"

"I swear," Jinx growls, making Kalen tilt his head in confusion. "Fucking strippers?"

"Fuck no," Kalen says. "McKenna would die of embarrassment."

"You said Collins," Jinx snaps. "I've killed a lot of men in my life, but never a cousin. It's not looking good for him though."

I nod in agreement.

Kalen laughs, shaking his head. "Some of the guys from the college were able to rearrange the furniture at Mom's house so they could have a team come in from the college to do a spa night. The girls get massages and a lot of pampering at low costs because the students need the experience."

I still narrow my eyes, and I can tell that Jinx isn't fully buying into it either.

"Are they all women?" my teammate asks.

"Does it matter? They're students and professional," Kalen says, defending the program as he's a math professor at Lindell University. "And if you still have doubts, their instructor will be there tonight as well. She and McKenna are good friends."

I take a deep breath, the first one I've been able to manage since I parted ways with Devyn.

"You've got it bad, man," Kalen says, pointing the tip of his beer in my direction.

I lift my beer up in mock salute, knowing there's no point in arguing the truth.

"Come on, assholes," Kalen says. "There are a couple of guys I want you to meet."

33

Devyn

"I can't believe this is the same park," I whisper, my eyes scanning the once open area to see all the chairs and decorations.

"Jinx said last night that they have so many events here. The whole town gets together every weekend for some type of celebration or fundraiser. Everyone gets involved. They help each other out all the time. The town is filled with genuine, kind people. It's sad that it's so uncommon that it seems more like a novelty, when in reality, the entire world should be like this."

I've never thought of world peace as a possibility. I'm young, well, younger than almost everyone at the clubhouse besides some of the little kids, but I grew up in a world full of active shooter drills and crisis scenario training. My childhood and Emmett's weren't the same. He went into the Marine Corps to experience the evil in the world. For me, and others my age, we witnessed it happening right on our doorsteps.

I squeeze into his side a little closer, grateful to have him and all those associated with him. I know Cerberus is here as a reminder of those who care for the people in this town. There were whispers last night of what had happened in Lindell. As much as they try to stay away from the troubles in the world, those problems still managed to infiltrate their small town.

"He looks so different," I say, my gaze pointed in Jinx's direction.

He's in a very nice, tailored suit rather than jeans and his leather vest. He holds his head high, proud to stand by his little brother while he marries the love of his life.

The ceremony hasn't even started yet, and I can feel the burn of tears behind my eyes. I know it's going to be beautiful and amazing. I also know it's going to leave me wishing I was the one up there vowing to love Emmett forever.

I look up at him and find him already watching me. When he cups my chin, I feel like I'm the only other person in existence. He makes me feel valued and loved, his actions speaking so much more loudly than words we haven't whispered yet.

"I think I'm going to cry," I confess.

Instead of making me feel silly for being so damn girly, he reaches into the inside of his jacket and pulls out a handkerchief. It's so old-fashioned but also somehow fitting for this sleepy little perfect town.

I clutch the fabric in my hand, standing when the wedding march begins.

McKenna looks stunning in her dress. No one in attendance would have a clue about her near meltdown when she discovered that her pet ferret had somehow managed to chew a small hole in the train. I was able to fix it and add some beaded and sequined detail down the back that covered the patch. She offered me her first-born child, but I declined with a laugh.

She only has eyes for Kalen. Even though I've been to a handful of weddings in my life, I never knew until now why some brides focus on their grooms and some look around the room.

She's lost for that man, utterly devoted. He's the only thing she sees, and with Emmett by my side, his strong arm around my waist, I fully understand.

She swipes at tears as they run down her soon-to-be-husband's cheeks when she steps up to him, and an echo of laughter rings out when the officiant clears her throat before Kalen can fully lean in to kiss McKenna.

"Let's get started," the officiant says. "The lovely couple seems eager."

There's another round of laughter before they exchange vows. I don't fully understand their references because I didn't meet either of them prior to yesterday, but many in the crowd seem to understand. It brings with it a sense of family and belonging.

Cheers go up when they're finally allowed to kiss, and my own cheeks heat at the way Kalen dips her back and ravishes her mouth like there aren't a hundred people watching it happen. They're in their own world, and good for them.

"Do you think..." I begin watching the newlyweds walk down the aisle and get chauffeured away in the back of an SUV.

"That they're going to have some—" he clears his throat suggestively. "Alone time? Yes. I want the same on our wedding day."

I stumble over my own damn feet.

We talk about the future all the time, but this is the first time he's flat out said we're going to eventually marry.

"Is this her?" a smiling man asks as he walks up to us.

"Devyn, this is Walker Conroy. He owns The Hairy Frog."

Walker takes my hand and attempts to lift it to his mouth, but Emmett's growl has him releasing me with a chuckle instead.

"This sad sap," he says conspiratorially, hitching his thumb at Emmett. "Sat on the barstool last night and pouted like a sad dog because he was afraid McKenna hired strippers."

I roll my lips between my teeth to keep from laughing.

Emmett doesn't deny it, however.

"I told him I'd have to look for you today to see the woman who had such a big guy all tangled up." He gives me a comical once-over, clearly not really checking me out. "Now I know what all the fuss is about."

I lean in closer to Emmett, pressing my hand to his stomach.

"Is this her?" Another man walks up, pulling a murmured curse from Emmett.

"Cash Tucker," the guy says, also holding his hand out. "I work for the Lindell Police Department."

"He's one of the only three cops in the department, a regular old Barney Fife," Emmett mutters, clearly annoyed that his behavior last night is being called out.

"Who?" I say.

Emmett looks to the sky as if he isn't surprised I don't understand the reference.

We chat for a little longer, and eventually Cash and Walker give up on trying to make Emmett feel bad for being worried about how I was spending my night last night. They chat about athletes and how many of the players people watch on television these days originated from Lindell University.

I'm familiar with some of the references, but not all. I've never paid much attention to any kind of sport. I've always been too busy sewing and finding other creative projects to work on.

When those guys split off, we start to mingle, and I notice when Mr. and Mrs. Alexander arrive back at the park. McKenna has changed into a different dress, one that's going to be much less cumbersome to walk around in on the grass. The day has ended up beautiful, the sun shining, but the chill of fall cooling it down enough that no one seems uncomfortable. It was a gamble for them to have an outdoor wedding this time of year, but it looks like it worked out for the happy couple.

Everyone is smiling and waiting patiently to congratulate the newlyweds. I imagine this is what perfection looks like. Kids are running around playing and having a good time. People are in small clusters catching up and sharing stories.

"I'm going to find something to drink," I tell Emmett just as he's starting a conversation about some first-class draft pick of something or other. I'm head over heels for the guy, but I'd never be able to stay awake if I stick around any longer.

"Want me to come with you?"

"No, no," I rush out quickly. "I'll be fine."

He shakes his head, that smile I've grown so used to seeing every day wide across his mouth.

"Hurry back," he urges before turning his head to argue with Walker about why a team in some league is better than the one the other guy picked.

I don't know how Emmett has had time to keep up with any sports recently. We've spent nearly every waking hour together the last couple of weeks. If I'm in my sewing room, he's always close by with an offer to help where he can. We have meals together, and by the time the sun sets each day, we're locked in his room and incapable of keeping our hands off each other.

"That is the smile of a woman in love."

It slides from my face the second Oracle says it.

"Is it that obvious?"

He tilts his head in confusion at my question.

"I don't want to scare him off," I mutter, feeling suddenly awkward and unsure of what to do with my hands.

"Scare him off?" Oracle snorts, the sound obnoxious and grating. "The man is head over heels for you. Anyone can see it."

My eyes scan the immediate area concerned Emmett might've finished his conversation and headed this way.

"What happened with you and that woman Beth?" I ask, wanting to change the subject. "Some of the girls were saying they heard you disappeared with her last night. They also said she's a little crazy and was probably planning your wedding before she got home last night."

"You guys haven't said it yet, have you?" he asks, rather than even acknowledging the things I heard about Beth Meyer, a local woman known for going all in after very brief encounters.

The groom made out with her once, years ago, and by the next day she had already registered for their wedding at a gift shop in town.

I glare at the man. "Why are you always in the middle of it?"

He holds his hands up, his playful smile vanishing. "What is happening right now?"

"You're trying to ruin this for me. Why?"

His head shakes. "Devyn, no. I'm just joking. Not about the whole love thing, that's like legit going on between the two of you, but just giving you a hard time about it."

My heart is pounding.

I know my reaction is over the top, but I also know it will be a very long while before I'll be able to fully stop listening to that voice inside my head telling me that Emmett will stop loving me. My parents did, and if the people who made you can do it, then anyone else can too.

"Is it something you want to talk about?"

I feel like the biggest asshole ever when he shrinks back at my glare.

"I didn't mean anything by it. Honestly, Devyn. I don't know you two very well, but I consider you both friends. I'd never try to get in the way of what you have with each other."

I nod, refusing to apologize despite my own feelings because I feel like they're valid. There are reasons I have to be so protective of what Emmett and I are building. As if it isn't enough that there's a twelve-year age difference. We have to contend with his own guilt over my brother's death and the fact that my parents will officially disown me when they find out about us.

He gives me one last pleading look before turning to walk away.

Forgetting my need for something to drink because of my need to find Emmett and be reassured that he cares for me, I scan the crowd. He's no longer where I left him, but coming up from the street are three men that clearly do not belong.

The ski masks are concerning enough but more so, each of them is holding a gun.

34

LEGACY

"He's not even a contender," I say, watching Devyn walk away, making sure she's out of hearing distance before switching gears. "What do you know about that whole Cortez situation?"

Cash switches gears just as fast. "I reached out to Angel Guerra who wasn't at all impressed that I had his phone number. He assured us that Raul Cortez is dead."

"And you have proof?"

Cash shakes his head. "He was reluctant to provide anything. The man's paranoid. Probably thought I'd try to bring some sort of criminal charge against him, but I wouldn't. A man like Cortez dying is a means for celebration."

I nod, quick to agree. Cortez is someone Cerberus has been battling against for the better part of a decade. He always managed to slip away and was quick to rebuild when Cerberus took down one of his houses. In the last year, he got involved with online sales, and his business grew. Depravity spread like wildfire because online users could spend their money from their basements or garages or wherever they felt comfortable paying to watch some seriously deviant things rather than having to shoulder the cost of an expensive trip out of the country.

"So we're expected to take the word of a money-hungry mercenary?"

Cash shrugs. "There are rumors that Guerra was one of his victims once upon a time, and that he had more skin in the fight than our little town, but who knows. What I do know is that we haven't heard a peep from anyone else. Well, not since Donavan held those Cerberus members hostage."

I could correct him because technically, he's wrong on several levels. Neither Landon nor Rick are members of Cerberus, and they were just a means to an end for him to keep an eye on Alani Warren. But honestly, that's just splitting hairs. Kid was livid that Landon was held along with Landon's husband Rick, but no blood was shed over that situation. Cerberus and the mercenaries went their separate ways.

"We appreciate you guys being here," Cash continues. "So don't take it the wrong way, but I think it's all in the past. There's no reason for Angel to lie to us."

"He's psycho," I mutter.

Cash nods. "I can agree with that, but we haven't had—"

A loud pop cuts off his words. I've been in far too many combat situations to confuse the sound of gunfire with anything else.

Cash reaches for his gun under his suit coat, and I do the same.

Several more pops echo around the park, combining with the shrill cries of the guests as they begin to scatter. Some are still standing around, confused about what to do.

I watch in horror as a man falls to the ground, blood blooming on his chest.

"There!" Cash snaps, the muzzle of his gun pointing toward the far side of the field.

My blood runs cold. It's the same direction Devyn walked a few minutes ago.

Another gunshot echoes, only this time it's the gunman who falls, his knees hitting the hard earth and the jolt ricocheting up his body until he slumps forward.

Before I can feel relief, more shots are fired, making it obvious that there is more than one shooter.

I can't tell who's hurt and who has hit the ground in an effort to stay safe. I lift my gun to fire at one shooter I've spotted but people are running everywhere. Firing without a clear shot could lead to me hitting a civilian. My mind is racing, unable to decide which is the lesser of two evils—to let him hurt someone else or shoot him on the risk of hurting an innocent myself.

My head isn't right, my fear that Devyn is hurt and bleeding somewhere, possibly dead, is jumbling everything up in my mind. I don't know how Aro and Slick work together and stay calm when they have to be worried about each other.

"Three down," Cash yells. "Do you see any more?"

I look around the area. The gunmen were decked out in all black clothing with masks pulled over their faces as if they thought they could come shoot up a fucking wedding and walk away without being caught.

People are still screaming and running. Children are hollering out for their parents. Several guests are injured, possibly dead or dying.

"I'm calling for more help," Hayes says, his face ashen white. He's a local firefighter I met last night at the bar.

My eyes continue to scan the crowd, looking for Devyn, but also keeping an eye out for Jinx. He's the highest-ranking member, the only Cerberus person here other than us newer guys. My military training urges me to find him because he'll have the answers. Before I can lock eyes on him, someone tugs my arm.

"Please," the woman says, her hands coated in blood. "Help him."

She grabs my arms, dragging me toward the man I first saw go down.

"Henry!" she screams as she falls to her knees, her hands covering the wound in his chest.

He's gone, and there's a good chance he was deceased before he hit the ground, but I won't be able to convince this woman that her efforts are useless. I know what it's like to try and save someone who can't be saved.

I rip off my suit jacket and drop to the ground with her.

"Apply pressure here," I tell her, wadding up the jacket and pressing it to his wound.

I'm not a medic, but the limited training I've received tells me the lack of active bleeding from the wound means his heart isn't pumping. She needs this. She needs to know she's done everything she could.

"Help is on the way," I assure her, my heart breaking for her loss.

I stand once again, the painful pleas in her voice begging him to hold on, telling him that someone will be there soon to help him.

I swallow against decade-old memories, looking down at my clean hands to prove that I'm not in the Middle East with my hands coated in my best friend's blood.

"Devyn!" I scream, but I know it just gets lost among all the others who are searching for their own loved ones.

A little girl is standing alone, screaming, although her cries don't reach my ears. On instinct, I move and scoop her up, holding her tighter when she realizes she doesn't recognize me.

I realize I'm running, holding this child to my chest like a lifeline. Others are more cognizant of their surroundings, helping the wounded, and organizing a sort of triage area. From the looks of it, the town has undergone some sort of catastrophe training. A woman is directing others on where to go, her voice too calm for her not to have had some sort of formal training and experience with emergency protocol.

"I found her crying," I say as I approach. "I don't know who her parents are."

The woman takes the child, cooing to her. "Sweet Reina, let's find your mommy."

Relief washes over me when the little girl drops her head to the woman's shoulder, her sobbing ebbing to hiccups.

I spend what feels like an eternity looking for Devyn and coming up empty. I walk the entire area more than once.

"She was right there with me," Oracle says. "I shoved her down, told her to stay behind the tree since the bullets were coming from the other side. I took down the one shooter and was maneuvering to get a shot on another one. When I looked back, she was gone."

He's shaking, the tremble in his hands matching the beat of my heart, unsteady and out of control.

"I've called in reinforcements," Jinx says, raising his voice when yet another ambulance takes off from the scene. "We have two shooters dead, and one injured and headed to surgery. We have two civilians dead and four more injured. Everyone is accounted for except Devyn."

"What the fuck aren't you saying?" I growl.

I watch Jinx's throat work on a swallow.

"One of the dead guys had a note on him that said kill all Cerberus."

My blood runs cold. "This was about us?"

"We aren't wearing our cuts," Stormy growls. "This was open fucking shooting."

"They had to be amateurs," Jinx says.

"Did we miss a shooter? Do they fucking know she's linked to us? Did they fucking take her?" My voice raises with every fucking question.

It's the only thing that makes sense. Devyn might have hidden to stay safe but once emergency services showed up, she'd come out of hiding to either look for me or help. She wouldn't continue to stay hidden.

"What's their connection to us?" Stormy asks.

"Is this Cortez related?" Oracle snaps.

That poor guy hasn't even been involved in anything related to Cortez and yet he and Newton are here getting fucking shot at for something that happened before he became a member.

"It's possible," Jinx says. "But Cerberus has been involved in a lot of takedowns."

We're responsible. Two civilians are dead and four are hurt because of us. What we do has bled into this tiny community, and we have blood on our hands because of it.

35

Devyn

I don't have to move to know my body is covered in bruises, but I guess I can't exactly demand I be treated with kind hands by the guy who dragged me away from the wedding.

I fought him like I remembered to do from every self-defense advice I've ever heard. I know the chances of surviving after being moved to a second location are slim. What they don't tell you is that as high as my adrenaline is at being abducted, theirs is just as high at committing the act. I grew slack, dropping all of my weight to the ground, but it didn't keep him from picking me up and carrying me along as if I weighed nothing. He easily overpowered me, yelling in Spanish as he tied me up and shoved me into the trunk of a car. I didn't have a hope of understanding what he said, and my pleas in English didn't faze him either.

I guess I should be grateful he didn't rape me, but I also know the trip isn't over, and that's still a possibility.

He's careless in his driving or at least it seems that way as I suffer even more injuries. He seems to hit every pothole in the state, each one ramming my body against jagged things in the trunk.

My entire body shakes in that way it would if I forgot my coat and had to walk a far distance to get where I'm going. If it weren't for the gag in my mouth, I know my teeth would be chattering despite the bloom of sweat generated by the unfiltered air I'm repeatedly breathing in and out.

I've never felt terror like I do now, but that doesn't stop my mind from cycling through my short lifetime of regrets.

I never told Emmett I loved him, although I've known I do for weeks. I didn't thank him enough for his generosity and willingness to share the found family he had in Cerberus. They welcomed me with open arms. Although I've expressed my graciousness for specific things, I've never thanked each of them for their kindness.

Em and Kincaid welcomed me into their home with limited questions asked. Em fought for me to open my business and helped me without reservations. Kincaid just smiled at me when Emmett made it clear I was with him. He even asked me if I needed help moving my things out of their spare bedroom when it became clear that I was going to be staying in Emmett's room with him. They didn't argue or try to talk me out of it. They never once judged the age difference or made snide comments. They fully supported me and the choices I made.

I scream into the gag when it feels like the car turns and ends up on two wheels. I slide against debris in the trunk, my head smacking against the side, my body crumpling with my neck taking the brunt of the jolt.

Tears sting my eyes, the dirt inside the trunk settling in them. I'm going to die in here, possibly from a car accident. My sobbing grows uncontrollable, my chest constricting until I feel like I'm having a heart attack. Breathing becomes unmanageable.

What if someone saw me get taken and someone is chasing after this guy? What if they get in a gunfight and someone shoots into the trunk?

I kick and fight as best I can, but the ropes and knots make it impossible to move. I can't even manage to move enough to knock out one of the taillights. It was suggested in a show I watched once. Apparently, if you knock out a taillight, it might alert a cop to pull the car over, but I know that's a risk too. This guy would never just pull over and act normal with me in the trunk. He'll just drive faster, more recklessly, and I'll die that way.

The car bumps along a little more, every sound amplified from the non-insulated trunk and the exhaust system right under me.

But then it stops. There was a crunch of gravel and then nothing.

I try to hold my breath as if it will somehow make the man forget he tied me up and shoved me in here.

Did I miss the car door opening? Did he climb out?

I can't hear much over the roar of my heart, the pounding in my ears drowning everything else out.

My mind races, flashes of what happened today infiltrating my head.

The man who fell beside me had unseeing eyes, the color draining from his cheeks faster than I ever thought imaginable. The screams, the children who were playing suddenly terrified and unable to find their parents. I tried to help one child, but the little boy wrestled out of my hands, and the guy who tied me up grabbed me before I could assure the little boy that he was okay.

I just knew I was going to end up like the shot man, dead and lifeless, eyes open, mouth agape.

Is that what war is like?

I sob as I imagine my brother's last minutes. Did he die quickly like the guy did today? Did he suffer? Did Emmett have to witness the color drain from his face?

The silence surrounding the car is louder than the road noise was. I know not to accept it as safety. There are worse ways to die than in a car crash, and even more pain involved when someone truly wants to hurt you.

My breathing calms as the silence continues. I try to convince myself that I'm safe, but then it hits me. This could possibly be worse than being dragged out of here and shot.

Slowly fading away due to dehydration and starving to death?

I rage against my restraints, trying to kick, and flail. I ignore the burns of the ropes on my skin. I know I'll have scars, but I can't just lie here and die.

I fight for what seems like a millennia, but to no avail.

The silence begins to feel like its own form of torture, and I'm certain that's what the guy wants it to feel like. I cuss him, scream every filthy word I can think of into the gag, imagining him standing outside of the vehicle and taking joy in my suffering.

Refusing to give him that sense of accomplishment, I calm, feeling as if it takes forever for my heart to slow. I won't give the sack of shit the satisfaction. If I'm going to die, I'll do so holding on to whatever dignity I can manage.

This sudden found bravery doesn't stop the tears. It doesn't stop me from wishing things were different, that I handled things differently in my life.

I'm going to die with too many regrets, too many words left unspoken.

I should've worked harder to make my parents see me. I should've reached out to Quincy more. I know my friend loves me. She's just living her life and making new memories, exactly like I've been doing. Getting busy isn't the same as discarding someone.

I do my best to shove down the pity party that's threatening its way up my throat. I squeeze my eyes shut, and try to think of the good times, the things I have to be grateful for.

Emmett is the very first thing that comes to mind, and I'm so happy I got to experience a part of my life with him.

I pray that Oracle was right, that the love he could see in my eyes was something Emmett could translate as well. I don't want to leave this earth with him doubting how important he was to me.

He spoke to me about losing Vaughn, and how he has spent nearly every minute of his life since avoiding any type of relationship, fearful of getting too close because of what it would mean if he lost someone again.

I pressed my lips to his jaw in that moment and vowed that I was safe, and that I wasn't going anywhere.

It looks like I'll be taking that lie to the grave.

36

LEGACY

"The oath I took," the doctor argues. "I can't—"

"Jason Conroy is dead because of that motherfucker," Walker growls, his angry finger pointing at the man in the bed. "A hole the size of my fist in his fucking chest."

"I can't guarantee that he's going to wake up."

"Just fucking tell us what to do so we can find that out?" Cash snaps from the shooter's bedside.

He looks seconds away from strangling the guy, and I don't fucking blame him.

"He may fucking know where Devyn is," I add.

It's been fucking hours since the shooting, and we still don't know where she is. Her phone was found under one of the picnic tables. None of the other shooters had phones on them. The only evidence we found was that fucking note about killing Cerberus.

Angel has been called, but he's still adamant that Cortez is dead and it's unlikely people are seeking vengeance for him.

Kincaid and some of the others are on their way, but the jet we took to get here had to go back to New Mexico to pick them up. Commercial flights would've taken even longer. They're expected here within the hour, but there's nothing we can fucking do if we don't get more information. There were no cars in town unaccounted for, so that means they all came in one vehicle. It seems that's the one the guy took who snatched Devyn up.

"I can't," the doctor repeats. "But if you just pull out that—"

Cash doesn't waste a second pulling things off and out of the guy, unconcerned for the dribble of blood when he yanks out the IV tucked into the bend of his arm.

The second all leads and wires are pulled away, Cash smacks the man in the face.

"That's not going to help," the doctor mutters. "You have to wait until the medicine in his system dilutes enough that he can regain consciousness."

The doctor leaves, his head shaking as if he's torn between the oath he took as a physician and the pain he's feeling because of the violation to his community.

I'm glad Cash isn't as concerned with the oath he took to protect and serve because I'd be doing exactly what he's doing if he tried to take the higher road.

We wait, the three of us taking turns pacing the end of the guy's hospital bed. Minutes turn into hours, and the piece of shit doesn't stir for over four hours, every second ticking by making my mind race with the things Devyn could be enduring.

I no longer feel like the hero many people claim Cerberus members are. I'm in that dark place where I'd destroy the entire world to make sure my girl is safe. I'd sacrifice myself, give up every memory I have of her just to ensure her safety.

I'm on the edge of no return when the guy grumbles, his face drawing up in pain.

Cash holds up his hand, blocking me when I go to grab the guy by the face.

"This is my fucking town," he snaps. "My fucking rules."

The fire in his eyes is the only thing keeping me from knocking his ass out. He wants to punish every single one of these guys for what they did, and I can easily tell he isn't going to take the fully legal path to make that happen. Vigilante justice probably isn't the way to go, and there will no doubt be repercussions for what we've done and will do in here today, but so be it. The jury of our peers were all just fired upon at an outdoor wedding. There's a good chance they'll be able to commiserate with us if it goes to trial.

Cash grabs the man by the chin, forcing him to look him in the eye.

"Where the fuck is she?"

The guy tries to jerk away, realizing quickly that he's handcuffed to the bed.

He refuses to answer, cussing Cash in Spanish, but Cash argues back, the language not as smooth from his mouth when he replies.

The guy shakes his head again, but is unable to rip free from Cash's hold.

"You'll fucking tell me one way or the other."

The guy's eyes widen when I hold the scalpel over his chest, using my free hand to rip away the flimsy hospital gown. I've seen some crazy shit, been witness to some torture techniques I'd never confess to seeing, but I've never been the one on the distributing end of it.

I press the scalpel to the outer corner of his gunshot wound without hesitation, wondering just how much the medicine still in his veins will dull the pain. He doesn't deserve an ounce of reprieve, but there's nothing I can do about what he's already been administered.

He screams with the first cut, fighting against Cash who presses a folded-up towel to his mouth to muffle the sound. His eyes are wide as if he can't believe someone would hurt him this way while he's in a hospital, a place meant for healing. The man shot and killed several people at a wedding, an occasion meant for celebration and love. The fucking audacity of this piece of shit makes me dig in harder.

"Let him speak," Cash says, pressing his hand against my forearm.

The guy whimpers and cries but he doesn't tell us anything useful.

I lift the scalpel once again, pressing it to a new area of his chest.

"Legacy!"

I jerk my hand, turning my attention to the hospital door.

I consider everything I can lose with the sight of my boss standing there.

"He has to know where they took Devyn," I argue, still unable to release the blade.

Nothing else matters if I lose her, and I'm fully willing to lose it all if it gets her home safely.

"He does," Kincaid quickly agrees. "I need to see you in the hallway. Mr. Tucker, Mr. Conroy, I'd like to speak with you as well."

I snap my eyes to Walker. Jason was his brother, and I somehow missed that during all of this shit.

Shadow, Hound, and Hemlock trade places with us, entering the room and closing the door as we step outside to speak with Kincaid.

"Let me say, Mr. Conroy, I'm so sorry for your loss," Kincaid says.

He nods, a vacant look in his eyes. I don't know how he stomached staying in the room with me without wanting to rip my eyes out. Those guys were there for us. The pain this community has suffered was because of Cerberus.

"Walker!"

I look around Kincaid to see a woman rushing toward us. I recognize her immediately as the woman who was crouched over the dead man in the park. She's still covered in blood, her hands washed but red still streaking up her arms. She's no longer in the dress she wore but in a set of scrubs no doubt given to her by hospital staff.

Walker pulls the woman to his chest, but she fights against him.

"Mom and Dad are here, and I don't know how to tell them," she sobs, making my throat threaten to close up with grief. She has to be their sister.

I take a step away, trying to give them some privacy.

"What was happening in there—" I say, attempting to explain to Kincaid.

"Was exactly what needed to happen, but I don't need that on your hands," Kincaid quickly explains. "There are others who are more adept at handling these types of things."

Before long, the hospital door reopens. I don't even have to guess who Kincaid was talking about when Hemlock walks out of the room wiping his bloody hands on a towel.

He doesn't look anyone in the eye as he walks away and disappears into the restroom down the hall.

"We have an address," Shadow says.

Walker whispers something to his sister that has her shaking her head and clinging to him as if she feels like she's going to lose him too.

"We'll keep him safe," Kincaid assures her when I honestly thought he'd refuse to let the man come.

Kincaid must understand that the man needs some closure.

"What is going on?" the doctor asks as he approaches. Instead of waiting for an answer, he scurries into the hospital room. "Jesus Christ."

The words are more shock than a prayer, but we don't stick around long enough to explain.

It takes an hour to get to the location Hemlock was able to cut out of the shooter. It's a meetup point of sorts, the place they all agreed to come back to if they got split up.

We approach the place with caution, decked out in the gear Kincaid and that group brought along with them. The guys who shot up the wedding didn't have assault rifles, but a handgun is no less deadly if given the opportunity for use. We dress the same way we would if we were going to war—full gear, and locked and loaded rifles.

I'm relegated to the back of the group which I understand for being so close to this, but it doesn't stop the rage from threatening to bubble over. I know the risk of going crazy and barreling in headfirst to a dangerous situation. I'm grateful for the trained men in front of me because I know they're just as willing to sacrifice their own safety in order to bring Devyn home safely.

"*I've got a parked car, but no movement,*" Shadow says from some vantage point none of us can see. "*There's no heat reading inside the house, but...*"

My hands are trembling so much I have to lower my weapon, the risk of an accidental fire real for the first time in my life.

"But what?" I growl into my mic.

"*The trunk of the car. Heat but no movement,*" Shadow explains.

There isn't a force strong enough to hold me back. I rush past Kincaid and the other guys, but stop just short of the car. I don't know what's worse, knowing or not knowing.

"Let me," Kincaid says, taking on the burden of pressing the trunk release of the car and walking back to the trunk.

"Boss," I whisper, the word a plea that holds more significance than it ever has.

"Thank fuck," he mutters, bending at the waist and reaching into the trunk. "Hey, sweetheart. You're fine. You're fine."

A whimper hits my ears, and it's the only thing giving me the power to move.

When Kincaid pulls her from the trunk, she looks like she's been beaten. She's covered in scratches, her wrists bleeding from where she fought against her restraints.

I step forward, pulling the gag from her mouth as gently as I can manage.

"Emmett," she gasps, her face streaked with tears, sobs catching in her throat.

"You're safe," I tell her, fighting the voice in my head that's reminding me she's in this situation because of me.

If she hadn't come to New Mexico, if I hadn't been so fucking weak, this never would've happened to her.

If I hadn't been obligated to the Marine Corps, if I hadn't been so willing to keep my family's legacy alive, Vaughn would still be alive. I'm the fucked-up connection in all of this. My selfishness made all of this happen.

"We're going to the hospital," I tell her, scooping her up in my arms and carrying her back toward the SUV parked out of sight.

Oracle offers to drive us, knowing the others will stay behind and scour the nearby woods, hoping to find the guy who deserted the car.

I keep her in my lap, a million questions in my head. I need to know how badly she's hurt, if that man had the balls to do more than what I can see on her skin.

I pull down her dress when it threatens to ride up.

"I saw a man die," she sobs. "One minute he was standing there smiling and the next he was just gone."

The other victim who succumbed was a woman, and that tells me that there's a good chance she was near where Jason Conroy fell. I don't know if the goal was to take someone all along or if the guy who took her improvised. The man in the hospital didn't give much info past where the meetup was before he passed out again.

I have no doubt we'll get more info later, but now that she's safe, the timeline no longer matters. Guilt swims inside of me as Oracle quickly covers the miles back to the hospital. She's in my arms and whole. Some people can't say the same about the ones they love.

"Did he...?" I manage before my throat seals shut.

She shakes her head. "He tied me up and put me in the trunk. That's all."

That's all.

Like she hasn't suffered possibly irreparable damage because of me.

"I fucking love you," I blurt. "I'm so fucking sorry I got you involved in this shit."

She shushes me, her hand coming up to cup my cheek. What kind of asshole does it make me that she's the one that faced god-awful trauma and she's the one comforting me?

She rests her head against my shoulder, and all I can do is thank my lucky stars that she's okay.

But the conversation we'll have to have tomorrow might just kill us both.

37

Devyn

I know I should be grateful for the care and attention I've received, but my attitude is flaring as we leave the hospital.

My diagnosis was bumps and bruises. The mention of the soreness on my head where I hit the side of the car was what I considered the worst of it, but I think I never should've mentioned it. It was diagnosed as a possible light concussion and they kept me in a private room for two fucking days before I got the discharge paperwork.

I know that had to do more with Emmett than anything else.

I saw on the news that one of the women who was shot was released yesterday. She. Was. Shot. And got an earlier release than I did.

I keep my discontent to myself as we walk outside because there are others who lost a loved one a few days ago. Although my feelings are valid, they're not as soul crushing as those who have lost someone.

Harper Conroy squeezes my hand just as I step into the sunshine. "I'm glad you're safe."

Her words are kind and as far as I can tell, genuine. Tears streak her face as she nods in my direction when I reach for her. It's as if she's trying to assure me that she'll be fine despite losing her brother. Her other brother, Walker, Jason's twin, pulls her into his chest, his eyes plastered above our heads as if he's trying to distance himself from all of it in order to be strong for his loved ones.

Emmett tightens his arm around me, guiding me toward the SUV parked under the porte-cochère. I want to pull away from him, remind him of the distance he's put between us over the last forty-eight hours, but the overabundance of armed men outside the hospital terrifies me. I know they haven't caught the guy who took me, but I'd convinced myself that he'd be running for the rest of his life.

I recognize the men and women from the clubhouse back in New Mexico, and I know their presence should make me feel safer, but it doesn't. I don't know if I'll ever feel safe again. I curl into Emmett's side and rush to climb into the vehicle once given the chance.

Every part of my body aches as Shadow drives us away from the hospital. I refuse to shut my eyes on the drive because every time I do, I picture myself tied up in that trunk. I can feel every jostle in my bones even with my eyes open.

Emmett places his hand on my thigh when I tense up. I wish there was more than just his need to protect me in his eyes. I keep silent once again.

It doesn't take us long to get to the hotel, but we're instructed to wait as others in the SUV pile out and take up position like they expect to be fired on. I wonder if this is what the president feels like every time he travels.

I ride up in the elevator with Emmett and Oracle. I feel more comfortable speaking in front of both of them.

"I doubt we need the entire Cerberus team here to protect me," I mutter.

"Half of the team is back home, making sure everyone there is safe," Oracle says. I watch as Emmett's jaw tightens, like he's not impressed with Oracle giving me this information.

My anger transitions from a low simmer to bubbling by the time Emmett closes us inside the room. Oracle takes a post outside the door.

I stare at the man who professed his love to me two days ago, but he remains silent.

I try a different tactic, walking toward him and running my hand up his chest. His eyes dart down to the bandages on my wrists before he steps out of reach.

"Are you fucking kidding me?" I growl.

"Now isn't the time for that," he says, unable to make eye contact with me.

"Not the time for comfort and assurance?" I challenge. "Because that's what I need from you."

"You're trying to initiate sex, Devyn."

I can't argue because I'm not above using sex to get him to get out of his head and to come back to me.

"One minute, you claim you love me and the next, you won't even touch me?"

"You're not going to fight your way into getting me to sleep with you right now! You got hurt because of me!"

He's loud, his anger clear, but I know it isn't directed at me. It goes deeper than that.

I snap my eyes to the door when I hear the knock. "Everything okay?"

"It's fine," I assure Oracle.

Emmett paces the room, his hands scraping over the top of his head.

"That fucking guilt you're feeling should be anger. *We're* not the problem, and it's ridiculous for you to even think we are."

He shakes his head as if he's rejecting every word from my mouth.

He walks around me when I place myself in his path, making damned sure he doesn't touch me.

"I will not just let you walk out of my life, Emmett Wilson. So you might as well hang that fucking idea up."

"You," he snaps, his face mere inches from mine. "Were hurt. Vaughn died because of me. Your parents hate me for it. I will not give them a reason to hate me more. You could've fucking died."

His voice is low and calm, his line drawn in the sand.

"Everyone at that wedding was at risk of dying."

"Because of Cerberus."

"Because evil men do evil things, Emmett. We can't stop living our own lives because there's a threat of danger."

He clenches his fists, breaths rushing past his lips. He's pissed, and he should be. I'm angry too. Harper was so kind to me while I was in the hospital. She brought me clothes and food, and cried with me, told me how sorry she was that I was hurt. The woman lost her brother, and she never pointed a finger at Cerberus. She never blamed anyone other than the men who did this for her loss. I don't know why Emmett can't take that same path.

"Everyone I love dies," he says, sounding more broken than before. "I can't, Devyn. I can't fucking love you. It's a death sentence."

I step in front of him, my back to the door to keep him from leaving when he walks in that direction.

"I get that you're upset and angry. I'll even give you the time you need to work through all that shit, but we're not doing this get angry, blame yourself, walk away, only to come crawling back later bullshit. I won't have it. So we're going to skip all that shit right now and just get to the making up part. You're fucking exhausted, and I am too. Take your fucking clothes off and get in the shower with me."

His eyes search mine, and I see it the second he accepts everything. Some of the shadows fade, some tension leaves his muscles.

"I love you," I say, hating the way he squeezes his eyes closed as if he has the strength to forget those words. "And I didn't survive all that shit just to end up lifeless because you walk away from me. You want to protect me? Then do that standing by my side."

It isn't much, but I see the slightest dip of his head, all the agreement I need for right now. We can discuss it further at a later time when we aren't feeling so raw.

"Help me with this," I say, turning around and pulling my shirt over my head.

"I hate all of this," he mutters, his fingers tracing the bruising on my spine.

I wince when he pulls at the bandage covering the worst of the wound.

Then I feel the warmth of his breath there, the slightest brush of a kiss, and somehow it feels better.

"The shower is going to hurt."

"I know," I answer. "But I'll be fine."

His eyes plead with me when I turn to face him, but I can't decipher what he's needing. I press my palm to his face, my own tears welling in my eyes when one rolls down his cheek.

"I love you," I whisper, catching one of his tears on the tip of my finger when he squeezes his eyes shut.

"Devyn."

"Forever," I assure him.

38

LEGACY

"I don't have any to spare," Devyn says as she hands over the soft fabric.

"I understand," I tell her, doing my best to hedge my smile.

"Just be careful."

"Promise," I vow.

She keeps an eagle eye on me as I lay out the fabric on her cutting table. Oracle and I have spent a lot of time in here in the last couple of days since getting home from Texas. With the wounds on her wrists from fighting her restraints, she's incredibly sore. When I saw her wince the first time she tried to use her rotary cutter, I demanded she stop and insisted the orders could wait. She argued about timelines, and this is the solution we came up with, supervised aid.

"Not that one!" she snaps when I pretend that I'm cutting on a different line than the one she needs. "You have to leave the seam allowance."

Oracle chuckles, knowing I'm joking with her.

She narrows her eyes at me.

"Now is not the time for that shit," she grumbles, catching on that I was only playing with her.

Instead of stopping what I'm doing and kissing her lips, I know what she needs right now is for me to do this right. The woman is quick to stress out when things don't seem to be going her way. I just need to accept that she'll be in my arms tonight, and I'll have plenty of time to *play* later.

She commends me the way she would if she were teaching a class when I get something right, and I've quickly learned to stop and ask questions if she gasps or gets a little twitchy.

"I've got that meeting," Oracle says as he finishes his own cutting project. He doesn't have as delicate a hand as I do, according to Devyn, so he's only allowed to work on straight line cuts.

"See you when you get back," Devyn says, giving him a quick smile.

We've all been ordered into counseling after we were debriefed when we got back to the clubhouse. At first, I wanted to fight against it. I felt fine, but when I told Devyn about it, she insisted that I go. It's not that Kincaid gave any of us an option, but I was planning to argue about it.

Devyn was quick to remind me that I tried to force her out of my life to keep her safe, and that was some shit I needed to work through because it can't happen again. She mentioned her fragile ego and the damage her parents caused with their negligence while she was growing up. She was very mature and told me she loved me but she couldn't keep wondering if I was going to leave her.

I'd do anything for this woman, and I'm beyond grateful that she stood her ground and didn't let me walk away. She was a hundred percent correct of course. I would've ended up crawling back because there's no way I could live without her. She even understood my position, that her getting hurt or ripped away from me is something I wouldn't survive.

I've vowed to keep her safe, and right now, only a few days after she was pulled from that trunk, it looks a lot like smothering and overprotection, but she's been a good sport about it.

"When is your appointment again?" she asks, knowing full well that it's tomorrow afternoon.

I know this is just her way of bringing up the subject.

I don't have a problem with Dr. Alverez. She's actually one of the better therapists I've spoken with. The ones required in the Marine Corps weren't bad, they were just overburdened and exhausted. It's hard for one person to provide adequate mental health services to the hundreds of people needing them.

"Tomorrow. I think this is ready for you."

I want to curl into her when she places her warm hand on my back and peeks around to the cutting table.

"I really appreciate you helping me."

"I still think you should take a break."

"Staying busy helps me cope," she explains. "It doesn't keep my mind from playing back every second, but it helps a little."

She takes a deep breath before returning to her side of the table.

"I wish they would've sent these in separate containers. It's a pain in the ass to have to separate them myself."

As much as she wants me to talk about what happened and how it makes me feel, she's as equally reluctant to talk about it herself.

"Could we order a different kind?" I ask, looking down at the pile of tiny beads she's planning to use to repair a wedding dress.

"It's fine."

I'd offer to help, but I tried that yesterday. The beads she's working with are so damn small, I can't even get my fingers to work the way they need to in order to sort through them without making a mess.

"What does your dream wedding dress look like?"

My heart is racing with the question because I can picture her walking down the aisle toward me, but in my head all I can see is her face. I don't care at all what she wears, just that the day will end with my ring on her finger and the echo of our vows in my ears.

"I haven't thought about it," she says, making my chest threaten to cave in. "Until recently."

Her cheeks flare with that perfect, sexy shade of pink as she lifts her eyes to mine.

"Yeah?"

She quickly pulls her gaze away.

"It's childish," she mutters.

"There isn't a single thing childish about thinking about our future."

"Our?" she whispers.

"Do you really think I'd let you marry someone else?"

She scoffs. "Let?"

I knew she'd have an opinion about that word. My attention these last couple of days has been rather smothering.

I step around the table, positioning myself in front of her.

"You're young," I begin, lifting her chin up with the tip of my index finger when she tries to look away. "Probably too young, but I can't live without you. I don't even want to try."

"I feel the same way about you. Not that you're young. You're rather ol—"

"Hush," I tell her, loving the sounds of her laughter. "I vowed to marry you when I turned thirty, and although when I did that it had nothing to do with you or who you'd become, I know now I was always meant to fulfill that promise. I had to wait for you."

"I'm glad you did," she whispers, her eyes shining with unshed tears.

"Thank you for loving me."

The first tear falls from her eyes.

"Always," she vows, and I know she means it.

My girl is a little broken, a little scuffed and scarred from her past, but I have no doubt she means exactly what she's saying. I don't just hear the words. I feel them so deep inside of me.

I press my lips to hers, wrapping my arms all the way around her, and drink in the warmth of her body.

In this moment, I give up on the thought that Vaughn wouldn't be happy about us being together. I know the man loved his sister, even on the days when she was getting on his nerves. He defended his country in an effort to keep them safe.

He could take one look at us and see how much we care for each other, how easily I'd lay down my own life to protect her. I don't think a big brother could ask for much more than that.

39

Devyn

Emmalyn is giving me that loving, motherly look. It's the same one she's given me many times in the six months since I showed up in New Mexico.

"You look stunning," Em says, a sparkle to her eyes that makes me wonder if she's going to cry.

I swear if she does, then I will, and Gigi spent too long on my makeup for it to be ruined so early in the day.

"Thank you," I tell her, pulling my eyes away as Em grabs a tissue from the box. I normally wouldn't have a box of them in here, but Oracle decided to try his hand at sewing last week and literally sewed his hand to a scrap of cotton fabric. He said it didn't hurt, but it sure bled a lot.

I lift my eyes higher on the mirror in order to see the door. My heart races when it opens and I see my mother standing there.

She gives me a weak smile as she enters the room. Emmett invited my parents, but I never imagined they'd actually show up. I figured I'd get hate mail at worse and at best, they'd ignore the fact that I'm marrying the man they claim is to blame for Vaughn's death.

When they arrived last night while we were rehearsing, I just knew it was to start drama, but they sat quietly, even chatted with Emmett's mom and dad. We didn't talk much. We never really do, but I guess it's good that they're here. I think I would've held a grudge if they didn't show up. I don't want to feel that way about my own parents.

"Do you want us to stay?" Em asks, her voice a low whisper.

I shake my head. I have no idea what my mother plans to say to me, but I'd prefer not to be embarrassed and have witnesses around if she gets nasty.

"I wanted to give you these," she says, stepping forward.

I look down at her hands, but I don't immediately reach for the dog tags in her grip.

I know the importance of them. I know how much she both loved and hated them. They were the reason her son was gone, but they were also one of the last things to touch him while he was alive. The dichotomy of that always made me wonder which side won out when they disappeared from beside the framed American flag she was given at Vaughn's funeral.

"Those are yours," I tell her, emotion threatening to clog my throat.

Her eyes reach mine, and I see the pain there. Her loss is as fresh as it was the day those men showed up on our doorstep to give her the awful news. It doesn't excuse the way she disappeared inside of herself when she still had another child to raise, but as a woman that now loves someone with their entire heart, I have a better understanding of what that loss is capable of doing to someone.

"I have to have them back," she says, her cheek twitching when she attempts to give me a smile. "You understand."

"I do," I tell her.

"I know he's a good man," she says, her hands trembling as she places the tags in my upturned palm. "He was always such a sweet boy."

"He's good to me," I agree. "He's an amazing human being."

"Vaughn just adored him."

She doesn't offer her own feelings about him, and I guess that might be too much to expect.

I'm not wearing rose-colored glasses. I know better than to hope that we'll work through all of our problems and that my parents will get involved in my life. If anything, this feels more like a goodbye than a mother trying to mend fences and fix what she's broken.

Oddly, I'm okay with it. I have this family here, and they've put no conditions on their love for me. I've been given the chance to mature and grow and succeed, all with them standing back and letting me experience life and learn from my choices.

"Thank you," I tell her as I wrap the chain around the stems of my flower bouquet. "I know it must be hard for you to be here."

She nods when a part of me was hoping that she'd argue, that she'd tell me it's not difficult to watch her daughter marry the man of her dreams, but that would be asking too much.

"You'll get those back to me?" she asks, her eyes glued to the tags hanging just below the cluster of hydrangeas in my hand.

"I will," I promise, knowing what's going to come next and hating the way that it's going to make me feel.

"We won't be able to stay for the ceremony."

I nod, biting the inside of my cheek so I don't speak my mind. It would serve no purpose, and would only hurt me more because I know it wouldn't change a thing. I keep my mouth shut to preserve my own peace, not to protect her feelings.

"Have a safe trip back to Nebraska," I tell her, turning away and looking back at my dress in the mirror.

I squeeze my eyes closed just as the door opens and closes, trying to accept that it may be the very last time I see my mother. My efforts are best placed elsewhere, namely working to build my life and future with the man I love.

I know my parents came because in their own way they needed to see that I was going to be okay. It allows them to fully wash their hands of me and not feel guilty about it.

I shake my head, taking a deep fortifying breath.

"They're ready," Em says, sticking her head back into the room. "Are you?"

"I've waited for this day all my life," I tell her.

Em gives me a quick hug before she hands me off to her husband.

"Thank you for this," I tell Kincaid as he smiles down at me.

"The pleasure is mine."

The president of the Cerberus MC, a man who has taken up a spot that's been missing in my life, walks me down the aisle where I marry the man of my dreams.

40

LEGACY

"It's supposed to be good luck," Stormy says, referring to the light spring rain that has managed to turn into a huge thunderstorm.

We were able to get through the vows before the sprinkle turned into a downpour, but no one in the room seems put out about the rain nor having to move the reception into the clubhouse.

"I'm not exactly upset about the way your dress is clinging to your body," I tell Devyn, my eyes dipping a little lower than they should while standing in front of company.

Her cheeks heat just like I knew they would.

"Would you stop?" she pleads, but there's humor in her tone.

"Do you two need a little private time?" Stormy asks.

"You mean more private time?" I ask, loving the way Devyn's mouth hangs open.

We spent a few minutes celebrating our nuptials just after the ceremony. I discovered that there's nothing much hotter than the way I bent her over the end of the bed with her dress still on. Even now, the threat of getting hard is very real because I know what I left behind on her skin.

She fans her face, trying to diminish the heat pooling under her skin. I fight the urge to do the same because there's nothing this woman does that doesn't turn me on these days.

Stormy chuckles, but lets his eyes roam over the crowd. There aren't many people here that I don't recognize, but I know everyone that is in attendance is on the approved list. Devyn's parents took off only minutes before Devyn walked down the aisle, but I guess it means something that they made the trip at all. When I sent the invite, I expected hate mail in return. They didn't say a word to me, although my mom and dad said they were cordial to them, avoiding nearly all conversation that was geared toward me. It's as if they were here to support Devyn in some fucked-up way but couldn't accept that I was involved. I realized long ago that I don't get to dictate how people act or how they feel.

After what happened in Texas, security around here has gotten tighter. The guy who took Devyn has never been caught, but we managed to determine that the attack was meant to be solely on Cerberus members. It makes it a little harder to not feel guilty for what the community of Lindell endured because of us.

It's common knowledge for anyone willing to do a little digging that Cerberus has its home base in Farmington, New Mexico, and that continues to put everyone here at risk despite the quiet over the last six months.

Several heads turn toward the door when the echo of the doorbell rings out over the soft music playing in the room.

Devyn stiffens, making me wonder if she thinks her parents will come back and stir up trouble, but I know that effort would be too much to ask for them.

Kincaid walks that way, checking the peephole before pulling the door open.

He blocks the person from entering, but the guy is extremely tall.

"This is about Janet and Carlen," Stormy mutters, having recognized the man.

I feel horrible for my friend. He got the call just a few days ago that one of his oldest friends, Carlen, and his wife, Janet, were found murdered in their car. They have no suspects, but Stormy has spent some time in their hometown in recent days.

Kincaid looks over at us, but rather than flagging Stormy over, he starts to walk in our direction with the man.

"Fuck," Stormy mutters. "What now?"

"Mr. Chilton," the guy says as he approaches.

"Mr. Dobbs," Stormy says, his tone reflecting his irritation.

"You missed the reading of the will."

He blinks at the guy as if he's confused. "They didn't have much to their name. I'm surprised they had a will."

"They did have one. It was older. It was done seven years ago right after their oldest son was born. It's the only one they had, so it's valid."

"Okay," Stormy says, shifting his weight on his feet as if he wants to run away.

"They named you the godfather, making you responsible for both kids."

My heart literally stops, and I jerk my eyes toward Stormy, waiting for his reaction.

"I'm no one's father," he says.

"There's someone else willing to take the children, Mr. Chilton, but the kids will have to go into care long enough for the courts to make sure the relative is safe and can provide for them."

His jaw tightens. "They only have two relatives."

"Correct, but Ms. Taylor is more than willing to assume the responsibility."

"The grandmother or the aunt?"

"The aunt," the newcomer clarifies.

"Like hell," he growls. "That woman is clinically insane."

"Let's discuss this in the conference room," Kincaid urges when Stormy bristles with rage.

"What the hell?" Devyn whispers as we watch them walk away. "Can you imagine?"

"Becoming a parent of two kids in the blink of an eye? Fuck no," I whisper.

"What about becoming a parent in general?" she asks, her teeth digging into her lower lip.

"We talked about that, baby." I cup her jaw and lower my mouth to her ear. "We can pretend all the time, but you're going to live a little bit of your own life before I make you a mother."

Her hands cling to me. "Can we go pretend right now?"

I feel the eyes of everyone in the room on my back when I pick her up and carry her from the room.

THE END

Marie James

MORE FROM MARIE JAMES

Newest Series
Mission Mercenaries

Lessons Learned
Mistakes Made
Bridges Burned
Depravity Delivered
Redemption Refused

Blackbridge Security

Hostile Territory
Shot in the Dark
Contingency Plan
Truth Be Told
Calculated Risk
Heroic Measures
Sleight of Hand
Controlled Burn
Cease Fire
Crossing Borders

Blackbridge Box Set 1
Blackbridge Box Set 2

Standalones

Crowd Pleaser
Macon
We Said Forever
More Than a Memory

Cole Brothers SERIES
Love Me Like That
Teach Me Like That

Cerberus MC
Kincaid: Cerberus MC Book 1
Kid: Cerberus MC Book 2
Shadow: Cerberus MC Book 3
Dominic: Cerberus MC Book 4
Snatch: Cerberus MC Book 5
Lawson: Cerberus MC Book 6
Hound: Cerberus MC Book 7
Griffin: Cerberus MC Book 8
Samson: Cerberus MC Book 9
Tug: Cerberus MC Book 10
Scooter: Cerberus MC Book 11
Cannon: Cerberus MC Book 12
Rocker: Cerberus MC Book 13
Colton: Cerberus MC Book 14
Drew: Cerberus MC Book 15
Jinx: Cerberus MC Book 16
Thumper: Cerberus MC Book 17
Apollo: Cerberus MC Book 18
Legend: Cerberus MC Book 19
Grinch: Cerberus MC Book 20
Harley: Cerberus MC Book 21
Landon: Cerberus MC Book 22
Spade: Cerberus MC Book 23
Aro: Cerberus MC Book 24
Boomer: Cerberus MC Book 25
Ugly: Cerberus MC Book 26
Bishop: Cerberus MC Book 27
Legacy: Cerberus MC Book 28
Stormy: Cerberus MC Book 29
Hemlock: Cerberus MC Book 30
Newton: Cerberus MC Book 31
Oracle: Cerberus MC Book 32
A Very Cerberus Christmas

Cerberus MC Box Set 1
Cerberus MC Box Set 2
Cerberus MC Box Set 3
Cerberus MC Box Set 4
Cerberus MC Box Set 5

Ravens Ruin MC

Desperate Beginnings: Prequel
Book 1: Sins of the Father
Book 2: Luck of the Devil
Book 3: Dancing with the Devil

MM Romance

Grinder
Taunting Tony

Westover Prep Series

(bully/enemies to lovers romance)
One-Eighty
Catch Twenty-Two

Made in United States
Orlando, FL
26 June 2025

62403272R00128